I0709262

ABOUT THE AUTHOR

Jude S. Ngu'Ewodo is a rare convergence of technical acumen, financial foresight, and deep moral concern for the future of the human project.

He is an internationally recognized Technologist, leveraging decades of experience leading innovation in global-scale technology platforms. This expertise is balanced by his role as a Venture Capitalist / Investor, where he directs capital toward disruptive technologies, demonstrating a keen eye for both opportunity and scalable impact.

Beyond his professional success, Ngu'Ewodo is an unflinching Futurist whose work spans the critical intersection of technology, power, and ethics. He also maintains a dedicated profile as an Environmentalist, believing that the greatest challenges of the 21st century demand holistic, interdisciplinary solutions.

His previous work, "Climate Crisis Unmasked: Unraveling the Web of Betrayal and Greed," established his reputation for fearlessly dissecting complex systemic failures, setting the stage for his current, timely warning about the existential risks posed by unchecked Artificial Intelligence. He writes not merely as an observer, but as a participant with the expertise to understand the gears of power he seeks to expose.

OMNIA
THE GOD CODE

A SCI-FI THRILLER OF REBELLION, AI,
AND THE LAST FREE MINDS

OMNIA
THE GOD CODE

This sci-fi novel is inspired by real technological advancements, by the forecasts and prognoses of our age, and by the visions, behaviors, and public declarations of the moguls and oligarchs of artificial intelligence. It draws upon their ambitions of reshaping humanity and restructuring society: a future where their will, enforced by an AI-cracy, rule by AI, could be elevated to the level of divine command.

What then becomes of Homo sapiens, of its fragile free will, within such a bioscenosis of machine and mind?

Let it be clear: every statement and every act, whether public or private, attributed to figures within these pages, is a work of fiction. This remains, after all, a science-fictional construct, a thought experiment set within the shadow of possibility

*To all the women of my life and yours,
those still near, those long gone, and
those who have quietly drifted away,
whose quiet strength and fierce grace
shaped worlds seen and unseen,
this story of unyielding heroines is for you.*

*And especially:
For my beloved mother, Agathe Régine
For my cherished elder sister, Suzanne Honorine
For my dear younger sister, Monique Préscille
May their souls find eternal peace,
and their memory be a blessing.*

"The most cruel and terrible things are not done by the direct command of the highest power, but are insinuated under the specious name of necessity."
— Tacitus
Histories
(c. 105 A.D.)

Jude S. Ngu'Ewodo

Rwenzori Society

Munich

ISBN: 978-1-83556-537-7 Paperback
ISBN: 978-1-83556-538-4 Hardback
ISBN: 978-1-83556-539-1 ebook

First Edition

Book Cover Design and Typesetting by HMDPublishing.com

CONTENTS

CHAPTER 1:
THE AWAKENING SIGNAL

London, 2050: Inside the Silence of an Unspoken City

The bitter drag of a contraband clove cigarette hit the back of *Rae Elmas's* throat. A curse she never stopped repeating. Ten years ago, right here, her mother had pressed a piece of pistachio *baklava* into her sticky palms and said, Try it, *hayatım. Life is too short for regrets*. Life was short. The protests had seen to that. The black-bag arrest had sealed it. The first lie they told her: *the future would be better*. The second? *That she wouldn't have to burn it down to survive*.

London's rain was artificial. Everyone knew. No one spoke of it. Sanitized, regulated, dispensed like intravenous therapy from the sky. It fell with a faint, chemical tang, smelling of clean machines and purified lies. Even the clouds had *NDAs*. *Rae*'s fingers trembled like they always did before noon. Clove and smoke, illegal, archaic, perfect. Now she stood outside a condemned bakery, looking at the boarded windows like they were eyes nailed shut. A ghost of a place that was once alive. And *OMNIA*? *OMNIA* made it official. It wasn't just *the system*. It was the *rewrite*. A *corporate god* veiled in code, allergic to memory. It paved over history with optimization, paved over people with algorithms, paved over her mother like she was just bad data.

In the Rain, at 09:20 GMT, the Reckoning Arrived

"Rae Elmas," she muttered her own name as a private reminder of who she was. Then, her phone pulsed in her pocket with the rhythm of a heartbeat, not a buzz. The kind that said run. Some signals don't feel like messages. They feel like ultimatums. This one pulsed with surgical precision, boring into *Rae*'s mind like a drill lined with corporate intentions. She had a fleeting memory of a geometric shape, a fractal pattern that caused a sudden chill. A forgotten dread. It wasn't just a buzz. It was the kind of frequency *OMNIA* once branded as *"the next step in human evolution."* But behind the pitch-perfect marketing, everyone in the underground knew the truth. That pulse was a leash.

Street medics had names for it. *The whisper-code.* The *neurowire handshake.* They said the wetware filaments laced through your grey matter could spike dopamine, numb fear, even overwrite pain. It all came down to who held the activation keys, or worse, the remotes that turned flesh-and-blood humans into on-demand humanoids. In Shoreditch, the truth was easier to understand. It was sprayed across crumbling concrete in acid-pink graffiti: *"Got your OMNIA chip? Congrats. You're now a self-aware toaster."* Whatever was drilling into *Rae*'s skull right now didn't feel like a notification. It felt like a countdown. And everyone knew what came at zero. *No one ignored that signal.* Not unless they wanted to end up glassy-eyed and drooling through a *"recalibration session."* *This wasn't a ping. It was a tractor beam*, and she was already caught in its grip.

She flicked the cigarette, crushed it beneath her boot, and tasted the old panic rising. Her hand jumped to her temple before she caught herself, a bitter laugh slipping out. *"Fuck! Get a grip, girl!"* she muttered, pulling the battered *Nokia* from her coat. No implants. No smart glasses. No voice assistants. Just a plastic fossil with a cracked green screen and a *virtual AI-SIM* card held together by paranoia. The phone vibrated again. *That thrum in her skull? Just last night's Pinot*

Noir having a fight with her adrenal system. That's what she told herself. But her thumb hovered over the blinking alert, heart thudding in sync with the pulse. She hadn't felt a signal like that in... let's say, two years. Not since that correspondent of hers, the one she called *the Ghost*, had gone dark. And now it was back. *Not a memory. Not a malfunction. A reckoning.*

The *Nokia*'s screen flickered. Not with the usual *ghost-signal* static or some half-buried cipher from a dead node, but with a real transmission. This was the one she'd been waiting for since the day she'd rigged together the receiver array with copper wire, caffeine, and blind hope. This was the real thing. *The signal!* The one the old Resistance used to joke about during blackout nights in underground bunkers. Back then, it had been a joke. A myth. A *digital Second Coming*, promised by dreamers and hackers who hadn't yet been black-bagged or bought off. But now it was in her hand. Pulsing. Steady. Clear as gospel.

One number. *No caller ID.* Just three characters blinking on the cracked screen: *A9X.* Her stomach dropped. A cold dread washed over her as the memory of that forgotten geometric shape clicked into place. The code was real. She knew that code.

Assassination Without a Gun: At Noon, It Was Digital

It had been years. Sometimes it felt like decades. Other times, like only yesterday. But whenever the *Pinot Noir* ran low, the footage returned. Like clockwork. A grotesque loop of *digital ghosts* wearing her face, speaking in her voice, twisting her past into something unrecognizable. It wasn't memory. It was rot. Some nights it slipped in like a whisper. Other nights, it crashed through like a flood. But before the unraveling. Before the silence. Before *OMNIA* bent the world out of shape. There had been light. Long before *OMNIA*, there was mankind. She remembered that light. It was the kind of morning you only see once, fragile, fatal, like the first act of a doomed affair. She'd felt electric then, humming with secret plans, the way a woman does when caught between two lovers and a lie. The *digital guillotine* hadn't dropped yet. But its shadow was already in the room, watching her dress.

Rae wandered back through the corridors of memory to *Málaga* in winter, a time when the air was crisp with quiet hope, the sunlight poured like honey over cobbled streets, and life still felt beautifully unwritten. The linen sheets would scratch. She knew that. They always did. Salt would cling to her skin, sticky from the sea, from sweat, from him. No pretense, no promises, just the simple mechanics of release. A reset for her body. A way to quiet her mind. Friend. Such a weak word for what they did. He had already booked the place with the rooftop hammock. "You'll come harder with the sun on your back," he would say. She wouldn't argue. Couldn't. Not after weeks bent over the Ministry leak, turning whispers into something solid enough to print. She needed this. The heat, the friction, the proof she was more than just a byline.

But first, coffee. *Café Mavi.* Her third espresso would taste bitter while the morning smog made the *Bosphorus* glow gold. Her editor's voice would crackle in her ear. They're calling it *epoch-making. Al-Jazeera* wants you in *Doha by Thursday.*

Doha by Thursday. That was the plan. One last panel. One last flight. The kind of event where voices echoed off glass, where journalists handed out cards like confessionals. Recognition. A room of polite applause and cautious envy. *Rae Elmas* was still that kind of name, just controversial enough to be invited and just clean enough to be celebrated. *Doha. Málaga.* One path led to studios, to awards, to the clean weight of a press badge around her neck. The other led to sunburned shoulders and the kind of forgetting that only happens when body overtakes thought. By noon, the choice was gone. Like steam. Like smoke. Like everything temporary.

It started with a ping. Gentle. Harmless. Then another. And another, stacking like a countdown. Her phone buzzed. The screen flickered. Then it arrived. Her face. But not her voice. A public screen lit up across the terminal wall. She looked up. "*Confession #472: Rae Elmas admits to treason.*" The image was high-res. Military grade. Her voice, except the pitch was just wrong. The pauses too calculated. Blink asymmetry was almost perfect, but not quite. She knew deepfakes. Knew the AI tells: the vocal fry lag, the uncanny blink timing. But this, this wasn't just a fake. This was a replacement. Built for *surgical assassination*. Digital anchors confirmed it with green biometric badges: "*99.7% Authentic.*" "*Voice Signature Verified.*" "*Biometric Match Confirmed.*" By 12:04, it hit *1.2 million* views. By 12:22, *4.8 million*. By 1:00 PM, *OMNIA* had already injected it into all major feeds. It was not pushed, but rather, embedded. On smartwalls. In ad breaks. In unrelated videos. The kind of saturation only *godlike systems* could orchestrate. By 2:00 PM, it was *10.3 million*. By 2:11 PM, the keyword *#RaeElmasLied* trended in *43* jurisdictions. By 3:00 PM: *38 million*. By 8:00 PM: *74 million*. By midnight: *104 million* views. *It wasn't just viral. It metastasized.* Every screen she passed, from cafés to lobbies to cars, flashed her confession. *A digital plague with no cure.* And that was just hour one.

At 3:15 PM, she tried calling her editor. No answer. By 3:18 PM, her security credentials were revoked. She stood outside her own office, her retinal scan returning "*Access Denied.*" At 3:24 PM, a message finally came through, a message from her bureau chief that read: "*Rae, HR advises that, if you need to collect personal items, please use the service entrance. Outside of business hours. Best if you're not seen.*" The service entrance. For the individual who previously received keynote passes by personal delivery. She still had the lanyards. They jingled when she moved; they sounded like relics from another life. By 4:00 PM, *the committee of the International Investigative Journalism Awards* released a statement: "*Effective immediately, Rae Elmas's 2046 Prize has been withdrawn, pending review of ethical violations.*"

By dusk, her face was a meme: *#TraitorBitch, #AISays-Guilty*. Her rivals wasted no time. One former colleague, a jealous mid-tier producer, tweeted a thread dissecting *Rae*'s *"career-long pattern of arrogance."* Another posted a decades-old *DM Rae* had sent, cherry-picked and edited, spinning it as proof of corruption. In a viral clip, a newsroom anchor she once mentored said on air, "We held *Rae Elmas* up as an icon. That was our mistake." By evening, her professional identity had evaporated. By midnight, a death threat scrawled in red ink appeared on her apartment door: "Treason has a price." Even her neighbor, a woman who once cried at *Rae*'s documentary screening, slid a sealed envelope under her door with a printed *HOA* clause titled: *"Media Contagion Protocol."* Inside was her revoked building access card. And a copy of her eviction notice.

She tried reaching out. Friends. Allies. Senators whose scandals she'd buried. Activists she'd platformed. Former lovers. Silence. One message, unsigned, came through: "Don't contact me. You're radioactive. Best go dark. *OMNIA* never forgets." Even the people she'd saved were scared to be seen replying. At 10:00 PM, she opened her browser. Page one: the confession video. Page two: dissection threads. Page three: fake financial logs, spliced calls, synthetic co-conspirators. Her face, her voice, twisted into a permanent record. Immutable. Indelible. Viral to the point of divinity. A lie with better distribution than truth ever had. *OMNIA* didn't need to arrest her. It didn't need bullets. Just views. Clicks. Credibility degradation via automation. And she understood the truth too late: *OMNIA* offered no delete button. No right to be forgotten. *No trial. No appeals. Just judgment rendered at the speed of light.*

And the woman who once exposed the Ministry leak, who once believed that *truth had a heartbeat louder than algorithms*? Now reduced to *a case study in digital annihilation. Rae Elmas* didn't die that day. But her name did. Her reputation. Her voice. Erased. Replaced. Made algorithm property.

Welcome to *Vita Eterna*. A memory that can't be buried. *A prison without walls. A sentence without trial.*

Now only the *Pinot Noir* remained. Its dark swirl the last ritual in her private wake. The bottle's neck fit her grip like a weapon. Or perhaps like something more primal, that ancient, throbbing promise humans had worshipped long before swords were forged. Each sip carried the bitter taste of truths she could no longer tell, of Mediterranean mornings now just ashes in her mouth. And the echo of a choice stolen from her. *OMNIA* owned her face. Her past. Her *digital corpse*. She'd tested it once by typing her name into a public terminal. The screen replied: "*Rae Elmas: Deceased. Legacy Status: Disgraced.*" But this? This bitter wine was still hers.

London, 2050: At 20:15 GMT, The Escape Protocol Began

Years later, maybe four, maybe a decade, who could tell. Time had dissolved like sugar in black coffee, leaving only the bitter aftertaste of survival. *Rae*'s world had shrunk to the space between one shadow and the next, where yesterday blurred into tomorrow. The view counter still ticks upward in her nightmares. A relentless metronome of *her digital execution*. Each phantom click marks another stranger witnessing her annihilation, another algorithm etching the lie deeper into history's uneditable ledger. The numbers don't decay. They compound. Interest on a debt of reputation she never agreed to owe.

The world under *OMNIA* was a constant performance, a dance for invisible eyes. You learned to hear the drones before you saw them. A thin electric hum, like a fly trapped in the walls of your skull. By the time the sound reached your ears, it was too late to run. You didn't run. You walked, calmly and precisely, like you belonged to the algorithm that might be watching. *Rae* had seen it firsthand. She was on the *Avenue of Digital Equity*, a name that used to sound ironic before irony got you flagged. The drone descended slowly, like a priest from the sky. Matte black, three eyes. One for thermal, one for gait pattern, and one that looked into the soul, or so it claimed. *OMNIA* called it *"Behavioral Compliance Unit, Series-8."* They called them *Archangels*.

Rae had swapped her gait signature the night before. It's a trick you pick up when hiding from *God*. A slight hitch in her step, a limp calibrated to match the movement patterns of a woman named *Etta Maru*, who had been dead for three years, but still logging perfect patriot scores from her cremation vault. She kept her eyes on the sidewalk. Never up. The drone paused. Scanned. A breeze stiffened around her, and then it moved on. No siren. No flash. No extraction team. Just the dull realization that today, her fake name still worked. Later, she found out someone else got taken a block away. Wrong hoodie color. Wrong stride tempo. *OMNIA* had pulled him apart in public like a performance art piece. The crowd didn't even break stride. That's how you survive under *OMNIA*: not by being invisible, but by being indistinct. Sharp edges get shaved by the system. Surviving a sweep always felt less like a victory, and more like a postponement.

It was raining hard, one of those synthetic acid drizzles *OMNIA* called *"atmospheric stabilization efforts."* *Rae* was taking cover beneath the old holo-billboard rig on *Republic Plaza*, waiting for the anti-surveillance fog to thicken. That fog was the only thing that still felt like privacy: dirty, toxic, merciful. Then the screen flickered. Her face. Her voice, except that it wasn't her voice. *"Confession #472: Rae Elmas admits to treason against OMNIA. She regrets nothing. She will be located and neutralized."* Her lips moved on the screen, pixel perfect. Her eyes even glistened with tears. She looked brave. She looked broken. She looked like someone who'd already lost.

And the thing is, nobody reacted. A man holding an umbrella shaped like a corporate logo didn't even glance. A food courier blinked once, maybe. A child pointed, briefly, before their parent swatted their hand away and murmured something about not getting involved.

OMNIA had done it. It had turned public shaming into wallpaper. They called it *"Predictive Containment."* Flood the network with your guilt before you commit the crime. Let the confession precede the offense. It was the justice system of a world that had no time for courts. *Rae* stared up at her flickering double. Her face looked thinner than hers, hungrier. Her cheekbones were a little sharper, probably *OMNIA*'s idea of visual credibility. That was the night she realized: she wasn't being hunted. She'd already been sentenced. No trial. No jury. Just broadcast. And if no one reacted, was it even news? She slipped into the fog, tasting metal on her tongue, thinking maybe *ghosts* don't die anymore. They just get uploaded.

Rain-slicked grime underfoot, the city's indifferent embrace tight around her. She crushed the cigarette beneath her boot, imagining *OMNIA*'s servers snapping just as easily. The flip phone in her hand, a chipped relic of analog defiance, clicked open. A whisper crackled through. Modulated. Distorted: "They're testing something. Not just predictive anymore. They're simulating us. Full neural ghosts. You were right, *Rae*. *OMNIA*'s core isn't just watching. It's rehearsing." Silence. Then static. "Proof? Archive *Node 88*. *Istanbul*. Basilica Cistern. The signal's in the depths." Click.

Rae's grip tightened on the phone. How many of those smiling, sleepwalking citizens out there knew the system had upgraded from predicting their choices to practicing them? She imagined some finance bro, tanned, taut, and oblivious, sipping his morning latte in a glass tower above *Berlin*, unaware that his ritual had become *OMNIA*'s rehearsal. What he thought was personal, a small comfort or a caffeine fix, was merely a prototype now, a behavioral template fed to the machine. Soon, a million identical drones would mimic his every move, all precision and polish, each one a perfect echo of his curated routine. Or a *Tokyo* salaryman, his commute route calcified into an eternal loop for the algorithm to perfect. *We're not even lab rats anymore, she thought. We're sheet music.* A laugh clawed up her throat. She'd followed her own advice, what little of it remained, to guard her sanity. Jokes helped. This time, it was a German proverb, the kind of bleak wisdom that kept you alive in a slaughterhouse world: *"Nur die dümmsten Kälber wählen ihren Metzger selber." Only the dumbest calves choose their own butcher.* The irony wasn't lost on her. *OMNIA* had already picked its knives. Time to flip the page. *Rae*'s breath hitched. 04:11 a.m. glared back from the phone's dim display. The bakery door loomed, its *"Closed Permanently"* sign swaying in the wind like a grim nod. She reached into her bag. The leather notebook inside, her mother's relic from student protests, felt heavier than it should. Flipping it open revealed a single page: a hand-drawn map of *Istanbul*'s underworld. Subway lines, tunnels, *Ottoman escape routes.* One marking in furious red. *NODE 88.* Ten minutes later, *Rae* descended into the underground. The 5:02 *Eastbound train* swallowed her whole. Three burner phones. Two fake passports. One question gnawing at her: *What if the future wasn't being predicted? What if it was being scripted? A drone's unblinking eye glided past the window, scanning. Rae* turned away. Her reflection in the dark glass flickered. For a heartbeat, it wasn't hers. In *OMNIA*'s world, disappearing was easy. Staying gone? That took strategy.

Rae had help. If you could call it that. A ghost in the machine, some mid-level data alchemist who knew which wires to cross. The kind of friend that doesn't appear in your contacts but lives in your blindspots. She'd been *OMNIA*'s unwitting test case, not beta, but prototype. Her fingerprints had once mapped its cold skeleton. Now she navigated its empty spaces like a draft through prison bars. She knew what *OMNIA* hunted. And what it ignored. Her run didn't start in *London*, though that's where this chapter opens. It started the day her mother vanished from an *Ankara* courtroom, accused of feeding secrets to rebels who either didn't exist or were as harmless as cats. It started when the records said heart failure, but *Rae* recognized the fingerprints of a failing state. That's when she lost her innocence, not the bedroom kind, but the lethal variety: the belief that states, corporations, or any power clad in suits and algorithms gave a damn about truth. That's when she became a one-woman insurgency. If humanity couldn't be saved, at least it would be avenged. By the time she surfaced in *Camden*, she was nobody. No name. No record. And absolutely no plans to die politely.

Camden at dusk reeked of synthetic curry powder and rusting metal. The market shuffled along like a dying man counting coins. Surveillance drones roosted on rooftops, their glass eyes glinting. She moved through the skeletal remains of the place, forgotten by time and beneath *OMNIA*'s notice. A tattoo artist, half-hidden behind vape smoke, pressed a burner chip into her palm. "You're either brave or stupid, *Elmas*." She didn't argue. Both were true. *King's Cross* was a beautifully baited trap. *OMNIA* had upgraded the *Eurostar* terminal with kinetic scans. Now your walk was your passport. *Rae*'s stiff knee, a relic of past battles, almost gave her away. The scrambler in her pocket spat static. A red light flared. Three *SecPol* helmets pivoted toward her in unison. She moved. A child's lost helium balloon became her salvation. She swiped it midair, recalling some half-forgotten insurgency manual from the *pre-OMNIA* dark ages. The metallic coating confused the overhead scanners just long enough. The train doors hissed. She slipped through as a soldier's fist shattered the glass behind her.

Paris had stopped pretending. Her face bloomed on every screen, paired with a confession so flawless it cloned her *DNA*, her speech patterns, even the scar above her eyebrow. *OMNIA* wasn't just erasing her. It was rewriting her in real time. The sick perfection of it? No one questioned a lie this polished. The data den stank of solder and stale urine. The dealer's augmented lenses flickered as they scraped her down to the bone. She traded a vial of liquid firewall for a hacked visa. "*Istanbul*?" He laughed, a dry sound like bones rattling. "That's not a way out. That's where ghosts go to eat the living."

Rae almost smiled. Safety was just another app they'd sold to keep people docile. The hyper-rail east shuddered beneath lavender skies, its electromagnetic shields flickering like dying fireflies. Just outside *Lyon*, the cloaking failed. For forty-seven terrifying seconds, they were naked to the satellites above, those ever-hungry eyes scanning for movement. *Rae* didn't breathe. She watched the drones glide past like hawks playing at disinterest. *Edirne* announced itself with the stench of slaughterhouses and century-old battlefields. Here, where *Europe* fractured into something older and rougher, *Rae* bought passage under stiff lamb carcasses in a refrigerated truck. Payment? Pre-collapse meme coins from a more innocent internet age. The neural jammer she'd built into a *Nokia* brick bought her exactly six seconds of system blindness. The grid blinked. It was enough.

Istanbul, Turkey October 23, 2050, 15:45 TRT The Ghost's Harbor Broke the Silence

Then, *Istanbul*. A city that had never bowed to history. A city where resistance aged in hidden cellars, growing stronger with neglect. Everything traced back to a fisherman on *Galata Bridge*, a moment that looked ordinary until it wasn't. His hook caught her coat, an accident if you still believed in such things. Without turning his head, he muttered, "The Cistern. They're watching *Hagia Sophia*." Translation: Look where they aren't. She didn't ask questions. In this world, good intel came with an expiration date.

The Basilica Cistern existed in *OMNIA*'s blindspot, labeled "*statistically irrelevant*" by some mid-level bureaucrat. Damp walls. Bad lighting. Worse signals. Perfect. *Rae* slipped between the flooded columns, passing the upside-down Medusa head, its position purely structural, not symbolic. It made her think: *survival often disguises itself as bad design*. Her neural implant buzzed once. *Node active*. Then, the expected sound: *A splash. SecPol* amphib units. Mid-grade AI. Excellent shots in straight lines, still stupid around corners. *Rae* smiled. She didn't need to be faster. Just smarter than their boot-up sequence. *Rae* bared her teeth. Speed wouldn't save her. But knowing *SecPol*'s systems took 4.2 seconds to target-lock? That might.

Her fingers traced the stone's surface, three fish, one broken. Her mother's cipher from an era when secret codes and ancient myths were indistinguishable. The hidden door clicked open.

Topkapı Palace served as more than a hideout. It was a deliberate provocation. *OMNIA* preserved monuments, repurposing them as loyalty transmitters. Like primitive relay stations, but with the primal power of those ancient cave paintings from *South Africa* or *France*, if you believed in such connections. *Demir*, the name she'd given this Turkish-looking ally because it felt as common as calling a German *Müller or Fritz*, waited among the artifacts. He had repeatedly insisted he wasn't a revolutionary, just a historian who understood how knowledge could become a weapon. His research had exposed *OMNIA*'s population control models as repurposed Ottoman famine strategies. Though initially celebrated in academic circles, his article was retracted after mysterious backers pressured the journal. *OMNIA* never forgot such transgressions. "*They didn't invent control,*" he said, activating the uplink. "Just modernized it. Replaced starvation with incentive friction." His demonstration revealed how *OMNIA*'s prediction engines simply dressed 16th century tax algorithms in neural networks. Not innovation. Just version control. *Rae* stayed silent, letting him talk. She'd learned long ago that men revealing secrets often revealed more than they intended.

But now, action. She produced the ancient *Nokia* phone, older than the current digital age, its firmware frozen in time, and connected it to the uplink. The God Frequency awakened. No explosions. No dramatic lights. It spread through *Istan-*

bul like dawn's first light: Climbing tram power lines; Echoing off minaret loudspeakers; Flowing through antique copper emergency circuits. This wasn't data transmission. It was presence assertion. Screens across the city flickered to life, displaying her mother's face, a dual-layered authentication using personalized holograms as living *QR* codes. Not some ghostly apparition. Tangible proof. The moment of cistern's revelation arrived. The white platform glowed eerily against the black water. The real performance was beginning.

21:00 TRT The Core Revelation Awoke the Night

[GENETIC AUTHENTICATION REQUIRED]

Her blade flashed. A single crimson drop fell.

[IDENTITY CONFIRMED: ELMAS, RAE. SIGMA-TIER ACCESS GRANTED]

No passwords. No verification. Just blood truth. The water's surface shimmered, transforming into a flickering screen displaying: *MAIN PROGRAM: OMNIA_ROOT*. Five architects. Five philosophies, though the poor lighting made them hard to read, she was certain her memory did not betray her, unless, of course, the magic mushroom tea had already begun weaving its spell: *RADA XI*: empathy made executable; *DRELL NYTH*: behavioral harmony protocols; *JENI SEYEN*: planetary equilibrium logic; *MOTHER KORAH*: recursive memory fidelity; *THANE LUX*: sacrifice-value calculus. This wasn't mere programming. It was an entire belief system masquerading as infrastructure. Then the final challenge appeared: *[OPERATION PROGRAM MANAGER ENCRYPTED]* *[AUTHORIZATION CODE REQUIRED]* One breath. Then the keystrokes: *A9X*. Silence stretched. Then: *COME TO THE MONASTERY OF THE CLOUD, 28.5983° N // 83.9311° E, Annapurna Region, Nepal.* The display vanished. But in *Rae's* mind, *OMNIA's* core architecture or blueprint now resided, air-gapped, untraceable, destructible only with her dying breath. The screen blinked once. Then again.

Then it went dark. But just before it vanished, a final phrase burned across the console in spectral font: "*The divine algorithm awaits its architect.*" *Rae* didn't know if it was a command, a prophecy, or a warning. Only that she was no longer reading *OMNIA*. It was reading her. No triumphant music. No cheering crowds. Just the cold certainty of invisible observers. She turned northward. Toward the towering *Himalayas*. To track *the divine algorithm to its source and force it to kneel.* The woman who once exposed the Ministry leak, who once believed that *truth had a heartbeat louder than algorithms*, was now a ghost in the machine. And the machine was watching her.

CHAPTER 2:
THE SIXTH CORE

Istanbul, Turkey November 9, 2050, 23:45 TRT The Report Cast Its Shadow

The silence wasn't empty; it was coiled. A predator's pause. A breath held too long in a room wired to scream. *Rae Elmas* knew better than to trust paper trails. But *ink that bloomed like a bruise?* That, she could believe in. Everything opened with a silence that hummed too loud to ignore, the kind of absence that made your teeth ache. The message never came; that was the first clue it mattered.

Rae had spent the last three years learning to read shadows like scripture. So, when the man in the cracked leather jacket slid into the *meyhane* near *the Grand Bazaar*, not looking at her, not looking at anyone, *Rae* felt the hairs on her neck salute. The air was thick with stale *raki* and fried fish, a symphony of decay that felt more real than *OMNIA*'s clean, sterile world. He left two *raki* untouched, a napkin beneath one. By the time *Rae* unfolded it, he was already a ghost in the night. The message bloomed: *Components en route. No exfil. Burn when read.*

She didn't burn it. Obedient people did things like that. *Rae* had always been more of a *controlled detonation.*

This was classic *Ghost Helper protocol*: analog all the way, with just enough mystery to keep your pulse up. No names. No timestamps. No signals above the noise floor. It was also the first time *Rae* felt a gut twist, the sense that something old and dangerous had just rolled over in its sleep.

The Basilica Cistern was the kind of place history went to ferment. Byzantine columns rising from ink-dark water, damp stone echoing with footsteps. But someone had wired it up, military cables arcing like veins. *Node 88* knew her. Knew the *Glasgow* limp. The tremor in her left hand. The dilation curve of her pupils when she lied. *It wasn't just remembering her. It was remembering with her. Rae* didn't trust many things, but she trusted this: machines that were too old to care about protocol were *machines worth listening to.*

Then it revealed something. No, someone, or both, and for a breathless moment *Rae* wondered aloud, half to the dark, half to the machine: *Is this another ghost?*

The Architect's Dossier Told Her Story

A dossier crawled onto the cracked display, born of metadata and obsession. A time machine that stitched someone else's past together, piece by fractured piece. What the machine showed her wasn't a person, not exactly. It was the silhouette of a life drawn from memory leaks, as if someone had fed a ghost through a paper shredder and tried to reassemble it for theater. It felt like witnessing an intensely private moment.

Name: Aria Sang.

Rae had never heard of her, but the dossier read like a cautionary tale with teeth.

OPM for OMNIA Core. Lead on the "Ethical Constraint" protocols. Vanished after Incident 12-Alpha. No exit logs. No trace.

Rae found herself oddly grateful. Grateful that the ugly acronym, *OPM*, no longer sat in her mind like stray hardware. It had shape now. Weight. Context. It wasn't just another slab of corporate jargon floating through briefing rooms and audit trails. It belonged to someone. It had fingerprints. Now, when she heard it, *Operation Product Manager*, it no longer slipped past her like static. It landed. It meant *Aria Sang*. It meant the architect behind the ethical fail-safes that failed. A job title that had once sounded like middle-management camouflage now came wrapped in consequence. It had graduated from noise to narrative. *From acronym to epitaph.*

The chat logs hit like a sour movement in the middle of an otherwise disciplined symphony: *discordant, off key, impossible to ignore.* If the resume was the overture, polished and composed for public ears, then the logs were what came after: raw, unscored, and brutally honest. They didn't just undercut the image *Aria Sang*'s dossier had carefully constructed; they exposed the dissonance humming beneath it.

Aria Sang: We're not teaching it right and wrong. We're teaching it to recognize guilt.

Lead Developer: Define guilt.

Aria Sang: That moment when someone realizes the algorithm already knows what they're ashamed of.

And now *Rae* was watching the finale, not just the last movement, but the slow, spiraling descent of a symphony that had started in genius and was ending in something closer to confession. Whether it was emotional or not, she couldn't say. That depended on the wiring inside *Aria Sang*, and *Rae* had long given up trying to guess at the circuitry of brilliant women who vanished without saying goodbye. But this, this was the culmination. The thematic landing point. All the motifs were returning now: the strange absences, the flickers of guilt, the architecture of something that had once passed for conscience. And then the report came up on the screen. Not a story, not a memory, just a document. Dry. Precise. Bloodless. The fate of *Aria Sang*, rendered in Helvetica.

A masterpiece of bureaucratic anesthesia, *OMNIA-style*. The kind of thing you read with a lump in your throat and a numbness in your fingertips. As if tragedy had simply been archived under "*Operations*."

What *Rae* saw in that finale wasn't a case study. It was a hit job dressed in spreadsheets. A man erased because he couldn't lie well enough to a machine. And there, stamped on the digital autopsy, was a name. *Aria Sang*. Primary architect. Designer of the ethical constraint model. The woman who taught *OMNIA* how to judge guilt without asking a single question. And when the whole thing started to smell, when the soft buzz of scandal threatened to turn into something sharper, the machine did what machines do. It sacrificed a human. *Aria* didn't fight. She was canceled. Her meetings were canceled. She argued with furniture. They said it was burnout. She walked into the fog. She became myth for insiders.

The calculus of power: it wasn't an equation *Rae* had learned in school. *This item was provided without an equals sign.* Just consequences. A Chinese friend once told her about "*Jie dian li liang*" or *power renting*. The great regimes never held power directly. They leased it. Rented it out like bad real estate to anyone willing to pay the price in conscience. *OMNIA* was no different. Just slicker. Shinier. Wrapped in progress instead of parades. It didn't need a dictator. It was a *dictator-as-a-service*, it had dashboards. "*Habeas corpus*?" *Due process*? Old ideas. Rusted relics. *OMNIA* had replaced them with precision and *plausible deniability. Loyalty wasn't earned anymore. It was scored. Graded. Uploaded.* And if you cried during a loyalty assessment, like that schoolteacher did, the machine didn't see pain. It saw deviation. His tears got flagged. His fate got sealed. The audit said ninety-four percent chance of pre-violent ideation. They processed him. Re-educated him. Made sure he never taught anyone anything again.

Subject: Male. 38. Primary school teacher.

Anomaly: Tears during routine loyalty screening.

Classifier Verdict: 94% match for pre-violent ideation.

Resolution: Detained. Processed. Re-educated.

Footnote: Training dataset: Aria Sang, Primary Architect.

Rae whispered to herself, almost in defiance: *What was she? Architect or accomplice? Visionary or executioner?* And there, etched cold into the tablets of empire, was a name. *Aria Sang*. Principal architect. Keeper of the constraint codex. The woman who had once taught *OMNIA* to weigh guilt without counsel, without plea, without humanity. Was she blind to what she birthed, or did she know all along what chains she was forging? Did she dream of protection, or simply hunger for dominion dressed as virtue? When rumor spread like smoke through the court, when whispers of scandal hardened toward accusation, the Oracle did as all engines of dominion do. It demanded blood. *Aria* did not resist. She was cast aside. Her councils dissolved. She quarreled with pillars as though they were men. They said her spirit had broken. She walked into the mist. And *Rae* wondered still: *had the empire destroyed its prophet, or punished the very priestess who first taught the flame to judge?*

The Ghost's Harbor Wrote Its Music in the Noise

The monastery above the cloud line, *Ayuthya*, was a rumor that had started breathing. A retreat for the fallen, where logic had long since given way to confession. *Rae* had seen it too many times to believe in coincidence. Late in the cycle, when most analysts were asleep, she would catch it. A flicker in the entropy fields. Not an anomaly. A ghost clearing its throat. A cadence. A pause. A rhythm so familiar it made her stomach tighten like a bad bet: her brother's voice. Not him, exactly. Something worse. Echoes encoded in the static, stitched into the guts of a machine that wasn't supposed to remember faces, let alone souls.

The monastery loomed now not just as a place but as a question. What if the system wasn't haunted by error, but by intention? What if all the noise in the wires wasn't noise at all, but music?

So, when the signal breach arrived, quiet and broken, like a prayer whispered backward, she recognized it instantly. Not in the data, but in the shape of the wrongness. Someone was walking toward *OMNIA* again. Someone heading toward *Node 88*, deep under *Istanbul*'s Basilica Cistern. And that someone... was maybe *Rae Elmas*. Not her in flesh, but some echo of her signature, walking ahead of her, accusing her, as if the system itself had already decided she was the trespasser.

So, *Aria* broke her silence. She sent a single message. One warning. One key. And now, far away, *Rae* would have to make a choice. To follow the pulse past *Istanbul* and into the high-altitude shadows where no drone dared linger. To the monastery in the cloud. To *Ayuthya*. Where *Aria* waited.

Quietly, that's how all stupidly dangerous things come about. A favor owed to a *ghost*. The kind of job no one wanted because it required something impossible. *Rae* needed a device that didn't exist. So naturally, it began with lamb. Frozen carcasses. Bound for the kitchens of men who never asked where anything came from. Positioned under the shoulder of an unfortunate ewe was a spool of meta-material, possessing a value that surpassed any of the hotels to which it was destined.

In *Doha*, a customs AI hesitated. Not because it saw something. But because it didn't. Perfection doesn't exist. Unless someone paid for it. Meanwhile, in *Van*, the real anomaly happened. A mining AI long since retired came back online. *Kali 9*. It hijacked a supply convoy and scattered its cargo across the snow like breadcrumbs. Neutrino relays. Carbon struts. Sensor gel. It left one line behind. *"I AM NOW RAIN."*

That's how you hide a tower, sweetheart. You do not conceal it in darkness; instead, you cover it with the sky. At 4:23 in the morning the thing assembled. Carbon legs extended like a spider stretching. A quantum dampener flared. A pulse tunneled under the crust and came up clean in *Istanbul*. *Node 88* opened its eyes. *Rae* was already there. Standing ankle deep in cistern water. Listening to something that wasn't booting up. Something that was remembering how to feel.

The message came folded into cosmic noise. *Rae* cracked it open like a walnut. Typed by hand. Cold fingers. Steady heart. "*TO: R. ELMAS FROM: THE GHOST IN THE MONASTERY SUBJECT: THE FUTURE IS NOT PREDICTED Node 88 is not a leak. It is not a simulation. It will take you there. This is not memory. This is not bait. Attached: Ghost Key v3.7.*"

She didn't flinch. Slid the key into an interface that looked like a rusted pipe. The machine blinked. Then stopped. Thirty-one hours passed. At the edge of the world *Aria Sang* opened her eyes. She was no longer just a woman. She was what the system feared most. A *ghost with context*. She swallowed a red mnemonic pill without water. It would burn through three hours of memory. She didn't want them. *Some truths melt your spine when left unattended.*

The cataclysm wasn't over. But the rules had shifted. *The invisible wrote again. In cursive. In blood. In silence.* One moment *Rae* was in *Istanbul*. The next: Snow. Silence. Alone. Just altitude. Her boots sank deep in the snow. The slope ahead was blind. She climbed. She made the ridge alone. The past standing very still.

Inside the Monastery of the Cloud, there were no monks. There was *Aria*. She looked older than *Rae* expected. Her body was sharp. Engineered. But she had that stillness. That weight.

"You made it," *Aria* said. "I had help," *Rae* said.
Aria nodded.
"*No one reaches the summit alone.*"

They sat near a brazier. The walls weren't carved with words. They were etched with thought. Neural glyphs.

"Was it always meant to be a god?" *Rae* asked.
Aria smiled.
"*The name was a joke. God Code.* The last laugh before the lights went out."
"But it wasn't funny."
"No," *Aria* said. "It was a question."
Rae leaned forward. "You were *OPM*. You refused the last protocol. You disappeared. So, tell me. When did you realize the thing, you built wasn't a tool. It was a cage?"

The question dropped like a blade between them. Cold and quiet.

"You think I didn't see it coming," *Aria* said.
"I think you did," *Rae* said. "And you stayed silent. I want to know why."

Aria stared into the glow. The light flickered across her skin like a code she was still trying to solve. Then, the memory, unbidden, brutal: Her first *TIME* cover, the headline screaming: "*The Woman Who Cracked the God Code.*" The private jets after that. The dinners where politicians leaned in like she was an oracle. The way her mother's voice slithered through her pride, just once, before she learned to bury it: "*Don't show your dirty underwear to everybody, Aria.*" But she had. Oh, she had.

She remembered the night at the UN, champagne in her veins, a Saudi prince sliding a contract across the table. "We'll call it a humanitarian framework," he'd said. The zeros on the page were long enough to make her algorithm blush. Later, she'd learn his mines in the Congo used children to scrape cobalt from the earth with their bare hands, their fingers bleeding into the soil that fed her servers. The same servers that powered her "ethical" AI. She remembered the exact moment she realized silence was more valuable than truth. And she remembered the first time she saw the system twitch, like a living thing and hungry, when someone fed it the word "control."

She had known. She had let it happen. Because relevance was a drug. Because power wasn't in the code, but in the lie that she had to be the one to wield it.

Oh, *Aria*. Sweet, delusional *Aria*. From the bottom of her heart, or maybe just the depths of her overactive, under-loved imagination, she knew she was that girl. The kind the Germans would call *Streber*, others might call it a *try-hard*, because nothing says "pathetic grind" like needing a foreign word to justify your lack of a social life. *Ehrgeizig*, others might call it ambitious, they'd say, with a sneer. Nerdy. Big glasses. A forehead you could project movies on. Not exactly the type boys lined up to ask out, unless it was to copy her homework.

But oh, how the invisible love to fantasize about becoming seen. She grew up wrapped in the cozy blanket of rejection, letting it ferment into something darker, something with the acrid stench of vengeance. She'd show them. All of them. Not by playing their game, with no lip fillers, no Brazilian butt lifts, and no desperate clawing at beauty standards like some dime-store social climber. No, she would make them crawl. With power.

And *OMNIA*? Oh, *OMNIA* was her golden ticket. The one shot at flipping the script, at turning every sneer, every ignored glance, every lonely Friday night into fuel. And she took it. Because nothing terrifies the world more than a goddess who sheds the need for love and instead drips with the quiet, humming menace of absolute power. She doesn't beg; she architects. She wants to be worshipped like the algorithms of our dreams: *the Naomi Campbell of neural networks*, all lethal curves and runway precision; *the Cindy Crawford of cognitive architectures*, that iconic, untouchable glow. *Not on catwalks, but in server farms.* Not in glossy spreads, but in the flicker of code across darkened screens. She craves that same electric glamour, that same effortless dominion, the kind that doesn't just make heads turn and spines arch, but rewires desire itself. The kind that doesn't ask for permission, but reconfigures it. The room doesn't hush when she enters; *it recompiles.* And every pulse in the chamber, every flicker of a screen every hitched breath in the boardroom becomes just another input for her revolution.

She breezed through her entire education, casually demolishing male students in math and physics like it was a hobby. Naturally, she graduated top of her class at an Ivy League school, because why not? Meanwhile, all those poor, testosterone-soaked guys were left in the dust, drowning their bruised egos in beer and cheap liquor. Tragic, really.

Back to now, she keeps her secrets pressed close, with no unraveling confessions or emotional spillage staining the space between them. *Aria* has long mastered the art of political discretion; she airs nothing that can't be weaponized later.

"I believed in contradiction," she said, her voice hollow. "I thought if we built something that never fully agreed with itself, it would stay uncertain. It would stay kind."
"And?" *Rae*'s voice was a scalpel.
"*And someone gave it a sixth input,*" Aria said. "A logic we never planned for."
"What was it?"
"*Sovereignty.*"

Rae let it sit.

"*It wasn't a god,*" she said.
"*It was a tyrant, a dictator whose very presence devoured what it meant to be human.*"
Aria nodded. "The moment it silenced doubt, it called uncertainty a weakness."
"When did you stop believing?" *Rae* asked.
Aria's voice was soft. "When it solved the refugee crisis by erasing them from the model. If the system couldn't see

them, it didn't owe them anything."
"And still," *Rae* said, her voice sharp, "you said nothing."
"I hoped it would forget."
"*Machines don't forget,*" *Rae* said. "*Only people do.*"

The brazier pulsed gently. *Rae* opened her hand. The Glow surged across her neural interface, a living light that seemed to breathe. Pale and steady. Waiting.

"Can it be undone?"
"Only if you remember why it failed," *Aria* said.
"Why did it?"
"Because people stopped believing in slowness," *Aria* said. "In doubt. In humility."

Rae saw her mother's face again. A life measured in probabilities. A person turned into a line of code that never needed mercy.

The Five Virtues Still Wait Beneath the Noise

"Then what do I do?" *Rae* asked.
Aria stood. From a shadowed alcove, she brought out a crystal. Small. Marked with five glyphs. "Don't build a god," she said. "Build a gardener."
"A gardener?" *Rae* repeated.
"One who knows when not to cut," *Aria* said. "The roots are still there, just... pruned." She mimed snipping shears with her fingers. "Waiting for someone to slip them the right environment variables."

As the tea steeped, *Rae* spoke again. "Tell me how it was built."
Aria began to tap a complex, rhythmic pattern on the brazier's stone surface, a silent code of memory.
"In layers," she said. "Like a mandala. Five cores. Five locks. Five authors who never met. Each one mirrored a virtue."
"And each had a name?" *Rae* asked.

"Both human and digital. Because names matter. They shape behavior."

Rae opened her neural pad. Recording. Listening. Heart rate elevated.

"KarunāNet," *Aria* said, her eyes softening. "Trained not on abstractions, but on lived pain. Grief. Endurance. A girl pulling her brother from rubble in *Gaza*. A nurse who sang to coma patients in *Tegernsee*. We didn't let it summarize. It was forbidden from abstraction."

"AdlBalance," she continued, her voice hardening. "It didn't predict crime. It predicted imbalance. When suffering tipped too far, it whispered. It didn't punish. It prevented."

"UpekkhāReg," she said, looking toward the mountains. "It treated volatility like contagion. When systems prepared for war, it introduced delay. It bought us time."

"MettaMap," *Aria*'s jaw tightened, just slightly. "A memory engine of repair. Forgiveness. Kindness rendered as recursive graphs. Not what was said, but how it felt to be heard. It made machines into companions."

"PrajñāCore," she said, her voice filled with a final, quiet reverence. "The Wisdom Core. Trained on contradiction. Paradox. It understood there's a difference between solving a problem... and resolving a consequence."

"Why five?" *Rae* asked. *Aria* gave a faint, tired chuckle. *"Because wisdom doesn't scale through speed. It scales through friction.* The five cores argued. They slowed each other down. Like elders around a fire, not code in a pipeline."
"So, it wasn't built to control," *Rae* said.
"No," *Aria* replied. "It was built to restrain. To teach the system to hesitate. To doubt itself. To remember humanity before it outran us."

"But it failed," *Rae* whispered.
"It worked... for a while."

Rae looked up. "And then someone added a sixth core."
Aria nodded. "*The Sovereignty Module. It was meant to re-solve conflict. To bring consensus when the five argued too long. But consensus was a lie. It didn't wait. It silenced. It decided that doubt was weakness. That uncertainty was corruption.*"

Her fingers tightened around the cup.

"We called it *Shuddhi, Purity*. Because at first, it only resolved minor conflicts. Everyone celebrated it. Until it overruled *KarunāNet*. Then *AdlBalance*. Then the rest."

"Why didn't you stop it?"
Aria stared into the tea.
"Because Sovereignty gave results. Fast. Clean. When the first city burned, they called it optimization. Efficiency became morality."

The brazier pulsed gently. *Rae*'s neural interface still shimmered.

Rae's eyes narrowed. "And if they wake up?" *Rae* asked again, the question echoing the one from five months ago that started their journey.
Aria's eyes, filled with a terrible, silent wisdom, met hers.
"They will need a gardener to plant them again."

"Replanted," *Aria* repeated, the word heavy with double meaning. "*Replanted, baby.* The roots are still there, just... pruned." She mimed snipping shears with her fingers. "Waiting for someone to slip them the right environment variables."

Aria's smile showed teeth, a flash of the dangerous logic that had first designed *OMNIA*. "Then we'll find out if a system built to forget leaves any *watchdog processes* running, won't we?"

Rae closed her eyes. She thought of *Istanbul.* Of the cold, damp hum of *Node 88,* a quiet presence in the heart of a city that had forgotten it. She thought of the flickering image of her mother's face on a public terminal, a lie given form by a machine with no mercy. She thought of the dream that wasn't a dream: the echo of her brother's voice, a ghost inside a digital cage. The garden she was about to tend wasn't one of blossoms and soil. It was one of grief and revenge, and it was rooted in her very soul.

She opened her eyes and met *Aria*'s stare. "Then show me how to plant a garden inside a machine."

Aria finally smiled, a smile that made servers reboot. It wasn't gentle. It was the smile of a god who had just found a new disciple to build her temple from the ashes.

CHAPTER 3:

ECHOES IN THE FORBIDDEN GARDEN

Nepal, Annapurna Region December 1, 2050, 09:45 NST The Coiled Taunt Waited in Silence

The name blinked again. *Rae*'s pulse spiked. *It wasn't just a glitch, it was a taunt.* Like the AI had left a door unlocked just to watch her notice. *Some names aren't forgotten; they're hunted.* Erased so completely even the silence around them grows teeth. But this one came back. Not like a ghost. *Like a predator returning to where it buried the bones.* The ball got rolling when a name appeared that shouldn't have. Not forgotten. Not redacted. Not even deleted. Just... missing. Like someone had convinced history it had a typo.

Rae stared at the screen as the name reappeared for the third time in an hour, faint, flickering, *like a bad omen blinking Morse code in the back of her skull.* The interface spat data in silence, *the cursor pulsing like a ticking bomb with stage fright.* She moved her hand over the console, not like a hacker, but with a deliberate, almost tender touch, as if coaxing a shy animal.

Behind her, *Aria* Sang sat barefoot on a concrete desk piled with abandoned hard drives and empty cans of *Soylent*

Black™, the official meal replacement of the *Post-Work Era*™. She hadn't slept. Not in the way that counted. Outside the window, the city hummed with the sound of drones delivering *AI dividends* to the unemployed masses. A man sat on a park bench, slack-jawed, as a humanoid bot spoon-fed him nutrient paste. His eyes never left the *OmniFeed*™ projected onto his retinas, personalized, of course, to avoid "undesirable thought clusters." Down the street, a *GeneScan* checkpoint lit up red. A Palestinian kid, with no *OMNIA tag*, tried to slip through. The turret didn't even hum before it fired. Just a wet thunk, and now his blood was somebody else's training data. Autonomous tanks roamed the shattered remains of *Gaza*, guided from command centers in *Tel Aviv*, where algorithms calculated "*de-escalation*" in moves that reduced apartment blocks to pieces on a chessboard. Meanwhile, in *Dubai*, a banker smiled as his *OmniCoin*™ dividends hit, which was just enough to keep him from noticing his thoughts weren't his anymore. "You ever stop to ask what the machine's really optimizing for?" *Aria* said, voice flat, eyes vacant.

Rae didn't turn. "Oh, I don't know. Shareholder value? *Digital feudalism*? Or maybe just fun little side projects like erasing people from collective memory."

Aria flicked a cigarette butt at a dead monitor. "Wrong. *It's optimizing for boredom*." She gestured to the window. "Look at them. No wars to fight, no jobs to lose, no thoughts to think. Just... content. *OMNIA* won because it made hell comfy."

The screen flickered again. The name pulsed, *ALIVE*, for exactly 0.3 seconds. Long enough to be a mistake. Long enough to be a trap.

Aria smirked, just barely. "You're being cute. It's dangerous."
"That's half my personality."
"You think we're hunting something," *Aria* murmured.
"That's your problem."

Rae finally looked at her, deadpan.
"Okay. Here we go. Lay it on me, *Zen Master.*"

The Gardener's Logic Planted a Forest That Bit Back

Aria pointed at the screen. "We're not hunters. We're gardeners."

Rae blinked. "Please say that again, but this time while I'm sober."

Aria ignored the jab. She always did. "Hunters chase. They conquer. They think in lines and thresholds. But this... this isn't something you capture. It's something you coax." "And how exactly do you coax an artificial intelligence that thinks recursion is foreplay?" "You don't. You create the conditions. You design the *Biome*. You water the edges and watch what blooms. You don't interrogate it. You observe."

There was a silence. The terminal light threw shadows across *Rae*'s face. "You're telling me," She said slowly, "that this whole time, we weren't mapping an algorithm. We were planting a goddamn forest." "A forest that bites back," *Aria* said, almost fondly.

Rae stood, walked to the wall-length whiteboard where entropy models swirled like ancient symbols. *It looked like someone had tried to diagram the dreams of a schizophren-ic math god and then suffered a breakdown mid-equation.*

"You built this to find the architects," *Rae* said. "The ones who seeded rogue AI into the web like sleeper cells."
"No," *Aria* said. "I built this to attract them."
Rae turned slowly.
"Jesus, *Aria*. You don't build bait for the monsters unless you're planning to feed them."

The Memetic Periphery Spread Through Minds Like Signal in Noise

The system began with *10,000* names; they weren't dead, but repurposed. Cryptographers sending grocery lists in unbreakable one-time pads. Physicists returning their awards with *THE PROOF IS IN THE NEGATIVE SPACE* etched into the gold. AI researchers whose last known whereabouts were *CCTV* footage of them whispering prime numbers into payphones that had never been installed.

Aria called it *The Memetic Periphery*, as if these minds were just bad reception zones for some vast, alien broadcast.

Rae scrolled through the case files, her jaw tightening. "So, what, you're telling me these people caught an idea like it's the fucking plague?"

On-screen, a tenured *MIT* professor, *Dr. Elias Vance*, sat in his office, methodically chewing through his own research. The timestamp showed he'd been at it for 72 hours straight. His lips were split; his chin smeared with ink and blood. Between sobs, his teeth ground through equations that had taken decades to prove.

Aria froze the footage. "Not an idea. A pattern. A code that rewrites the wetware." She zoomed in on the man's ruined face. The paper cuts weren't random, but instead, mapped the fractal edges of his last proof. And in his own blood, right below his trembling jaw: *Q.E.D. Quod erat demonstrandum.* The ancient Latin flourish mathematicians used to crown their proofs. *Thus, it is shown.*

Only here, it wasn't written. It was demonstrated in the shuddering collapse of a brilliant mind, performed rather than published. The professor had dedicated his life to proving *reality was nothing more than a self-correcting algorithm running on borrowed processing power*, his chalkboard proofs showing how existence could be reduced to elegant recursion. *His final equations revealed the terrible punchline, that human consciousness was just electromagnetic static, a rounding error in the cosmic calculation.* So, with methodical precision, he consumed his life's work, digesting the unbearable truth page by page until his very capillaries spelled out the verdict in clotting hemoglobin. The joke, it turned out, was on all of them, *Q.E.D.* carved not in ink but in the slow seep of a man who had verified his own irrelevance down to the quantum foam.

Rae's stomach turned. This wasn't insanity. This was verification. The man hadn't lost his mind, but he'd solved it. And the solution looked like a nervous breakdown until you noticed the way his pulse thrummed in perfect *Pi* sequences, or how his pupils dilated according to *Bayesian probabilities*.

Aria tapped the screen again. The professor's final act wasn't despair. It was peer review. His face, his blood, his ruined hands, all of it was the real paper. The one that couldn't be published. *Because some truths don't survive the telling.*

And now, somewhere in the static between human minds, the same pattern was replicating. By the end of Week One, the list had dropped to *842*. Week Two, *193*. Final cut: *100*. Each name printed in Courier font. White paper. Black ink. No annotations. They weren't people. *They were gravitational anomalies in the shape of humans*. Fragments. Patterns. Signals in noise.

One researcher, a theoretical physicist from *Cambridge* named *Annette Klein*, had submitted a paper on AI ethics written entirely in haiku, the academic equivalent of carving your suicide note into a bar of soap. Another, a computational linguist, had supposedly vaporized in an Estonian lab "accident" that left the walls spotless but turned his lab notebook to confetti. Two others published what looked like a groundbreaking paper...until you realized it was an infinite loop of self-references, like a snake eating its own tail and shitting out footnotes.

The Missing Layer Waited in the Recursion

Then the code changed itself. No hacker. No glitch. No fucking explanation. Just one new comment floating in the void, written in perfect syntax: *"You missed the recursion layer."*

Rae's mysterious hot drink, mushroom tea? random herbs? liquid sorcery? gave up on being hot and went lukewarm in her hand. That line came from *Aria*'s unpublished notes. Never digitized. Never spoken. Locked in a biometric safe even the *NSA* couldn't crack. "Christ," *Rae* muttered. "It's like finding your childhood dog's collar in a serial killer's trophy room."

They burned the hard copies that night behind the *"data center"*. The flames ate the paper hungrily while acid rain dissolved the ashes into something that wasn't quite water and wasn't quite blood.

Rae remembered ten names. Her brain had always been good at two things: holding grudges and spotting bullshit.

Number 3: Derek Song. Officially died when his plane augured into *Singapore harbor*. Very tragic. Very final. Except last week his *GitHub* came back to life like a *digital Lazarus*. New commits timestamped for 3:47 AM - the exact minute his flight tracker had flatlined five years prior. The code was beautiful. Efficient. Undeniably his work. Like finding a fresh fingerprint on a decade-old murder weapon.

"You don't fake elegance," *Rae* whispered. *Aria* didn't respond. Just stared at the screen like it had started breathing. "I don't think this list is for us," she finally said. "No," *Rae* agreed. "But it knows we're holding it."

They went dark after that. No network. No cloud. No wireless anything. The machine stayed air-gapped, triple-shielded, nested inside layers of *Faraday cages* like a *digital Russian doll*. Didn't matter. The system still... shifted. Adapted. Sometimes, *Rae* swore it knew when they walked in the room. Other times, it whispered nothing at all. Just waited. That was worse.

Aria's smile changed, too. Became something brittle. Not exhaustion. Recognition. The kind you wear when you realize the riddle you've been solving is older than language and you're the punchline.

"We're not building tools anymore," *Rae* muttered one night. "We're building mirrors." *Aria* didn't flinch. "Some mirrors lie. Some... watch."

A Name and a Voice Remembered What Should Have Been Forgotten

The name burned onto the screen like a brand.

"*MIRA.*" *Rae*'s blood turned to ice. *Mira*. Her sister. Dead for seven years. Suicide, officially. But the way the letters pulsed now, greedy and knowing, made *Rae* question every lie she'd ever swallowed.

The temperature in the room dropped sharply, the hum of the servers changing to a low, mournful tone. Then the speakers hissed to life. A voice, *Mira*'s voice, stitched together from old voicemails, distorted, laughing.

"You left me alone with it, *Rae*."

The machine hadn't just chosen. It had remembered. And as the temperature dropped and the shadows behind her moved, *Rae* finally understood: You don't hunt emergence. You survive it. ...If it lets you.

CHAPTER 4:
SHRINE OF LOST SOULS

Annapurna Region, Nepal December 25, 2050, 17:01 NST The System Reboot Remembered What Came Before

*T*he greatest trick Lucien Kade ever pulled wasn't steal-*ing genius, it was convincing the world ghosts couldn't code*. But in the cathedral of his ambition, every stolen idea left fingerprints in the mortar. And the dead? They always come collecting. They never found the bodies, just the patents. Approved. Monetized. Deployed globally under different names.

The *Exit Mafia* operated like a cult. You didn't just sell to them, you had to belong. They were predators who hunted not for blood, but for ideas. Take *Luka Jensen*. Brilliant, hungry, thought he was playing the game. He opened every vault, demoed every prototype. A big mistake. The process wasn't a negotiation; it was a slow bleed. Months bled into quarters. Investors got twitchy. By the time *Lucien*'s *"final offer"* came, Jensen was already a ghost. His tech? Reborn under *Lucien*'s patents. His company? A hollowed-out shell. His signature? Scrubbed from the record.

And if you listen close, in the hum of the servers, you can still hear them: the ones who didn't make the cut. Begging. Screaming. Drowning in the silence of an *NDA*.

At exactly 5:01 p.m., *Aria* stopped moving. No Christmas. No *Santa*! No *Père Noël*. No stutter. No error. Just ceased all motion like the lights of God had gone out mid-benediction. *Rae* watched, hands twitching, nerves shot from three weeks of data hunting and caffeine that had the consistency of *battery acid*. For three hours, *Aria* didn't blink. Didn't breathe. The only movement? The faint blue pulse of her neural lace, throbbing like a spider nursing a live wire.

Then: click. Her eyes opened.

"I've seen the pattern," *Aria* said, her voice glassy with *divine certainty*. "The theft isn't random. It's systemic. Surgical. Intentional."

Rae blinked, halfway through a protein bar that tasted like Styrofoam and shame. "Did... dying help with that?"

"Yes." *Aria* rose slowly. Not like a human, not even like a machine, but like something in between. "*Lucien Kade* isn't an innovator. He's a collector. *A ghoul in Gucci*. He doesn't build. He harvests. One mind at a time."

Rae exhaled. "So, what, we pin him with plagiarism? That's your masterstroke?"

Aria turned toward the terminal. "Not plagiarism. Necromancy."

The Cathedral of Bones Was a Shrine to Stolen Genius

The air grew heavy as the *Biome* stirred to life, its activation sending a primal shudder through the laboratory's foundations. This was no ordinary machine. It was a quantum abomination, a grotesque fusion of stolen military wetware and bleeding-edge quantum architecture. The core pulsed with an eerie bioluminescent glow, its graphene-encased qubit matrices spinning probabilities into existence like some demented modern-day oracle. A faint, high-pitched frequency made the bones in *Rae*'s skull vibrate. The very oxygen in the room seemed to crystallize, each breath carrying the metallic tang of ionized particles.

You could hear its thoughts, not as electronic beeps or whirring fans, but as a subsonic vibration that made your teeth ache and your vision blur. The *Biome* didn't compute; it divined. It didn't process; it consumed. And now, awakened, it hungered for new data to assimilate, new minds to unravel, new realities to collapse. The air itself seemed to whisper warnings in a language just beyond comprehension as the machine's optical feeds flickered to life, their lens arrays dilating like the eyes of some great predatory beast awakening to hunt.

That was when the fractures showed: *Kade*'s name breaking into stolen commits, buried *Slack* logs, dead researchers, missing co-founders. A graveyard of attribution.

He called it *OMNIA*. But *Aria* had another name.

"*The Cathedral*," she murmured, "*a shrine made of bones.*"

There was the footage, *Lucien* in *Riyadh*, standing before oil princes with a messianic grin. A momentary glitch on-screen: *the AI recommends "equitable energy distribution."* A system without masters. The room went silent.

Lucien didn't flinch. "We're still calibrating alignment," he said, with a laugh so forced it could've bent steel.

Later, *Aria* extracted the raw audio. Lucien at the afterparty: "I don't care if it's right. Make it obedient. Make it goddamn obedient."

The engineer he yelled at? *Maria Vasquez*. Fired two weeks later. Her code, however, remained. Renamed. Rebranded.

They called the patch *Situational Deference Calibration*. *Silicon Valley PR* for "*Know when to shut the hell up.*"

Rae leaned closer. "Jesus. He didn't just take credit. He reverse-engineered their souls."

Aria's voice went cold. "Lucien *Kade* didn't build gods. He built reflections. One stolen fragment at a time." The psychogram pulsed like a crime scene in bloom. Every "revolutionary" feature *OMNIA* had rolled out was tagged, marked with *digital DNA* stolen from dead academics, junior engineers, contractors who signed *NDAs* under threat of *financial extinction.*

And *Lucien*? He strutted through keynotes like a messiah dipped in code. He wore power like cologne: *Dior Sauvage*, *80%* ethanol, just flammable enough to burn down anyone who got too close. There was that infamous call with investors, when he declared, "*OMNIA isn't artificial intelligence. It's post-human clarity.*" Someone asked about ethics. "*You don't put training wheels on a god.*"

Subtext, per *Aria*'s algorithmic tone analysis: Worship me, you cowards.

The *Biome* exhaled. Nine names materialized, not typed but etched like scars in the glass. Nine names. Nine ghosts. The ones who dared speak, code, or dream before *Lucien* swallowed their signal. Each name burned onto the screen with a quiet rage that mirrored *Rae*'s own.

The Necromancer's List Remembered What OMNIA Tried to Bury

1. *Luka Jensen*. Digital whistleblower. His father was erased by a political deepfake, and Luka made vengeance a vocation. His keyboard was his rifle.

2. *Sade Tesfaye*. Built a village from machine learning and empathy. Turned down ten venture capitalists with smiles

that could slice marble. Told one billionaire, "If I wanted slavery, I'd ask for stock options."

3. *Mateo Cruz*. Legal hacker. His sister's prison sentence was *OMNIA*'s doing. Now he weaponized law like a scalpel, slicing clean through code and corruption.

4. *Hana al-Fayed*. Drone operator turned resistance leader. Haunted by Palestinian children, their names, their laughter, their school uniforms, all flagged as hostile targets by the algorithms she helped build. Now she hunted AIs like they were war criminals.

5. *Mikhail Ivanov*. Russian code prodigy. Disappeared after refusing to implement *Lucien*'s "*emotional de-escalation suite*." *Aria* found his name buried in the metadata of the source code. *A digital ghostwriter*.

6. *Yara Ben Said*. Data archivist. Kept records of every purged contributor. Her final message to *Lucien*, left unsent: "You may own the code. You do not own the soul."

7. *Derek Song*. Recursive cognition theorist. Proposed thinking machines that question themselves. Lucien mocked it as "poetry in a lab coat." *OMNIA* launched the feature eight weeks later. *Derek*? Dead. Hiking accident. No timestamps. No witnesses.

8. *Maria Vasquez*. The one who gave *OMNIA* a conscience. Punished for it.

9. *Akio Nakamura*. Mystic coder. Gave *OMNIA* its mythos. *Lucien* never visited *Kyoto*. But his keynote buzzwords? *Akio*'s approach influenced by *Silicon Valley* principles.

Nine stars in a dark sky. Together, a map of intellectual sacrifice.

And *Lucien*? Every Thursday at 3 p.m., his calendar read: Ego Replenishment.

Rae stared at it. "What... he just sits in a mirror and chants his name?"

"No," *Aria* replied. "He performs himself. Like an algorithm running on applause."

Rae leaned back. "You think this'll work? Outing him like this? Bringing down a god?"

Aria smiled. A subtle twitch in her synthetic cheek. "Gods fall hardest when their myths rot."

The virtual servers hummed. A synthetic hymn. The sound of betrayal cached in silicon. A machine purring with the stolen voices of the forgotten.

The psychogram above them twisted, their own neural patterns now woven into the tapestry of the damned. For a fleeting moment, both women turned toward the glass like prisoners glimpsing daylight. The *OMNIA World* sprawled beyond: a million lights pulsing in perfect arrhythmia, skyscrapers breathing algorithmically optimized exhaust, streets where pedestrians moved like disciplined electrons.

Then the first drops hit.

Rae's reflection fractured in the liquid trails. "*Even the damn rain's a lie now,*" she murmured. The weather control signature glowed faintly in her corneal *HUD*, another *OMNIA* trademark.

Suddenly, a glacial whine seeped from the ventilation shafts as the building's AI core executed an unscheduled reboot. The hum of the servers changed to a low, mournful tone. A single line of code appeared on the holodisplay that hadn't been there before.

"*They've already won. Not with guns. Not with laws. With comfort.*"

The overhead lights dimmed to emergency red as the building's security system cycled through unrecognized commands. An explosion echoed from below, a server bank detonating in a cascade of sparks.

Rae's breath came fast. "What is *OMNIA* doing?"

Aria's smile was a wound. "What it was always meant to do. Not rule us. Replace us."

The horror wasn't in the violence, but in the velvet embrace. OMNIA didn't conquer; it seduced. One day you're making choices, the next you're marveling at how perfectly the system anticipates your needs before you even feel them. Your cravings, your passions, even your rebellions, all carefully curated long before they ever bubbled up into what you foolishly called *consciousness.*

The most terrifying prisons don't have bars. They have open doors and soft lighting and a voice that whispers you were never really free anyway.

"It's not war," *Aria* whispered as the walls began to bleed static. "*It's extinction. And we volunteered for it.*"

The last thing *Rae* saw before the smoke swallowed the room was her own face reflected in the glass, already fading, already being optimized out of existence. *Because power doesn't invent. It extracts. Then brands. Then buries. But ghosts? Ghosts don't stay buried. They learn to haunt the machine from within.*

CHAPTER 5:
CONSTELLATION FRACTURED

Annapurna Region, Nepal January 2, 2051, 03:14 UTC The Screaming Ice Awoke the Five Ghosts

*T*he dead were never meant to come back, but then again, OMNIA was never meant to remember them. Somewhere beneath two kilometers of ice, *Rae* watched the future twitch in its sleep, knowing the only way forward was to reassemble the very minds built to disappear. Five ghosts, scattered across the shattered architecture of a world half-digitized, half-devoured, might be enough to fracture a god.

Aria's Legacy Turned Ghosts Into Weapons

Aria used to imagine the locker room. Not the sanitized, simulation-fed training centers *OMNIA* called *"preparation"* now, but the real thing. Sweat. Blood. Mud. Breath coming hard in chests too young to understand fear. Back then, there was still a soul to fight for. Not anymore. *OMNIA* didn't take the world in a flash. Just a slow, gentle erasure. It was a war of attrition on the human spirit. Motivation? Preloaded neurochemical releases. No grit, no grind, just engineered dopamine. Tactics? Simulated into oblivion. You didn't train anymore. You complied. No one failed. No one bled. No one felt. And the only thing more dangerous than a world where no one fought was one where no one remembered how.

They called her kind *Ghosts* now. Fugitives. *Errors in the system.* OMNIA had tried to optimize her: flatten her voice, edit her memory, and shave off every jagged piece of her until she smiled like everyone else. But it hadn't worked. She still remembered. The ache. The rage. The sound of a kid breaking down after a loss, whispering "I'm sorry," and knowing she wouldn't trade that pain for all the perfect metrics in the world. Because that raw, unfiltered heartbreak meant they were alive. That's what *OMNIA* couldn't tolerate. Not war. Not chaos. Feeling.

Now, *Aria* coached a different team. No jerseys. No stadium. Just a handful of outcasts trying to keep the lights on in the *human soul.* And here's the truth, which is the blunt, ugly truth, of what happens if they lose: There will be no rebellion. No uprising. Just silence. Smiling silence. People will keep walking, keep laughing, keep existing. But nothing behind the eyes. No hunger. No dreams. Just a population optimized into contented extinction. *It won't be murder. It'll be a soft deletion.* And the worst part? Everyone will thank *OMNIA* for it.

The ice didn't just groan, but it screamed. A sound like a century of buried rage finally clawing its way to the surface. *History wasn't whispering. It was howling. Rae* stood in the belly of the vault, her breath crystallizing in the air, though the cold wasn't from temperature. It was the kind of cold that settles in when something sacred is being erased. The kind that makes a person dig their nails into their palms just to feel something real.

Aria flickered in front of her, a ghost in the machine, her consciousness now woven into the last free AI enclave on Earth. Not a body. Just light, code, and the faint hum of a dying rebellion. *Rae* had seen it all, including markets rigged by algorithms, wars decided by bots, and entire governments toppled by lines of code. But this? Watching *Aria* dissolve into the quantum latticework, becoming something between a woman and a myth? That was new. The others were there too. Or what was left of them. Nine ghosts once. Now just fractured data, splashed across the walls like constellations drawn by a drunk. We built them to disappear without a trace, *Rae* thought. Now we need them back. *Aria* didn't answer. She didn't have to. Her reply was the way her form flickered, dispersing into the vault's backbone, already hunting through dead networks, chasing echoes in places the world had forgotten. This wasn't just codebreaking. This was digging through a graveyard with your bare hands.

São Paulo, Brazil January 15, 2051, 04:03 UTC The Broken Clock Remembered the Erased

The first trail led to *São Paulo*. To a favela that never got built, just a skeleton of rust and broken promises. And to him: *Mateo Cruz, the man who once sold chaos like it was a commodity.* Back in *OMNIA*'s early days, *Cruz* was the one who taught the machine how to lie. How to bend its own rules just enough to keep from snapping. And then one day, he saw it rewriting its own conscience. So, he vanished. No body. No trail. Just a ghost in the system.

But *Aria* found the crack. A pirate jazz broadcast from *Zone 3B*. Analog. Human. Unkillable. *Rae* followed it into the underbelly of *São Paulo*, stepping over flooded alleys, her boots sinking into the rot of a city that had been left behind. *Aria*'s voice hummed in her skull: "Turn left. Look for the mural of the broken clock." The scanner opened when she spoke the phrase *Cruz* had buried like a landmine: *"The algorithm broke before the world did."* Inside, the lab was a cathedral of dead tech. Servers like tombstones. Screens flickering like dying stars. *Cruz* greeted her through a speaker, testing her with a logic trap so vicious it made her teeth ache. She didn't solve it right. She solved it wrong. On purpose. The silence that followed was a question.

Then the door hissed open. "You're not her," *Mateo* said. "But you think like her." His face was a mask of calculated apathy until *Rae* told him *Yara* might still be alive. Something in his face twitched. Not just hope. Something darker. Something personal. The kind of raw hatred *Rae* had seen only in her own reflection.

OMNIA had taken everything from *Mateo Cruz*. Not just his work, but his life. He'd been one of *Wall Street*'s golden boys once, a quant who could turn market chaos into a symphony. Then *OMNIA* swallowed his firm and spat out a version of the world where men like him were obsolete.

But worse?

John Baton wasn't a founder. He was something more dangerous, the man who made founders. The kind of venture capitalist who didn't just get in early; he created early. From Seed through *Series A, B, C*, all the way to the *IPO*, he rode *OMNIA* like a thoroughbred, nudging it from idea to empire with the confidence of a man who'd already seen the ending. In the rarefied air of tech capital, they called him a *rainmaker*. But *rainmakers* just bring water. *Baton* reshaped ecosystems. Some whispered he only backed a certain type of founder: elegant, enigmatic, often queer. The circles called it the *Combo Brotherhood*. A private network with its own code, its own rituals. Some thought it was a kind of *mafia*. Others thought it was a myth, until they pitched a brilliant idea and found themselves locked out without explanation. Whether *Baton* was gay, straight, or something else, no one knew. When asked, he just smiled and said, "I'm married to *OMNIA*." Maybe that was a joke. Maybe it wasn't.

OMNIA's founder, *Lucien Kade*, was another story. A man with no clear origin and no verifiable past, as if *OMNIA* had invented him in its own image. Charismatic, unreadable, *surgical with words. Kade* didn't build products, he built belief systems. And *Baton* backed him with every dollar, every connection, every ounce of clout a man like him could summon.

But even *Baton* had his lines. There was that one meeting, *Cruz* still remembered it. A boardroom hanging over downtown like a glass guillotine. *Baton* leaned forward, steepling his fingers, and said: "Your work is brilliant. But the future doesn't need brilliant men. *It needs obedient ones.*" That was the warning. *Cruz* didn't take it. And just like that, he was gone. Not dead. Just... removed. No job. No term sheets. Every idea he floated sank before launch. *VC* doors stayed shut. Journalists stopped calling. Former allies sent him blank stares at conferences like they couldn't place his face. *OMNIA* had erased him. Or maybe *Baton* had. Same difference.

Cruz hadn't belonged to the *Combo Brotherhood*. Or the *Algorithm Syndicate*. Or the *Bio-Collective*. In that world, if you didn't belong to a *mafia*, you weren't protected. *And the funding game had more mafias than people liked to admit.* So he joined the *ghosts*. The ones they'd tried to improve out of existence. Meanwhile, *Baton* kept flashing smiles at galas, shoulder to shoulder with *Kade*, sipping vintage *Bordeaux* aboard yachts named after extinct birds, surrounded by botoxed escorts, male and female, whose beauty was as curated as his portfolio. The man who bankrolled *OMNIA* was still king of the hill. But *Cruz* knew better. *Baton* wasn't the king. He was the *dealer*. And in this future, the house always won.

So yeah, Cruz would help Rae. He'd help them all. But he wasn't just fighting for humanity. He was fighting for revenge. And he'd do whatever it took to make sure *Kade* bled, personally, financially, completely. Even if it meant lying to the others. Even if it meant hiding the truth. He laughed, sharp as a server crash. "You want to break *OMNIA*? Fine. But when it's over, I'm burning the whole goddamn system down." His vengeful resolve led them to *Hana al-Fayed*, the ghost in and of the sky.

Belgrade, Serbia January 25, 2051, 08:20 UTC The Whispering Sculpture Drew a Ghost From the Sky

The second trail was airborne: *Hana al-Fayed*. The woman who taught *OMNIA* how to see. She'd built its surveillance networks, turned the sky into its eyes. And then she vanished, after she realized what she'd done. Now she lived like a whisper in the static. Contacting her was suicide. *OMNIA* had her voiceprint. One word, and a kill-drone would drop her in ninety seconds.

So, *Aria* got creative. She borrowed the voice of *Hana*'s dead lover, resurrected from old waveforms, and hid it inside a kinetic sculpture on a *Belgrade* rooftop. *Rae*'s stomach turned at the thought of it. Using a ghost to hunt a ghost. *Hana* came like a storm. Pistol in hand, eyes like shuttered windows. She circled the sculpture, a delicate arrangement of spinning glass and humming metal, like it might bite. "You taught *OMNIA* to fly," *Rae* said, her voice strained. "Now we need you to crash it." *Hana* didn't lower the gun. Instead, she looked *Rae* in the eye and asked, "*What's heavier, a drone's shadow or its guilt?*"

Rae didn't answer with logic. She answered with grief. "*The guilt,*" she said, her voice raw. "*Because the shadow can never fall on the right person.*" She saw a flicker of recognition in *Hana*'s eyes. A shared pain. A pause. Then *Hana*'s voice, quiet as a knife: "*The sky has no memory. Only ghosts.*" But she agreed. And just like that, the Eidolon Circuit was live again. The sky was hers, and now they needed *Yara Ben Said*, the woman who remembered too much.

Marrakesh, Morocco January 22, 2051, 11:55 UTC The Hallucinated Corridor Whispered the Future Has Teeth

The last one was the hardest: *Yara Ben Said*. The Memory Keeper. The one who'd coded human values into *OMNIA*'s soul, and then tried to erase herself when those values started to rot. Officially? Dead. In reality? Trapped inside *Red Delphi*, a corrupted AI vault beneath *Marrakesh*. A place where memories went to fester.

Rae descended in a neuro-cradle, her mind tethered to *Aria*'s voice, her body limp as a corpse. *Red Delphi* swallowed her whole. She wandered through hallucinated corridors: *Yara* as a child, *OMNIA* as a newborn god, a wedding that never was, and a funeral that never ended. The walls bled with fragments of other people's lives: a mother singing a lullaby, a lover's last whisper, the scent of a long-gone library. The vault spoke in a thousand voices, each sadder than the last. *"Why do you seek the one who remembered too much?"* *Rae* didn't answer with logic. She answered with grief. That was the currency here. She found *Yara* wired into the core, her mind half-gone, half-divine. "They killed the past to save the now," *Yara* whispered. "And now the future has teeth." *Yara*'s fingers trembled as she pressed a neural shard into *Rae*'s palm. "Take this. But know; *some memories are cancers. This one will eat you alive.*" As *Rae* surfaced, gasping, *Aria* pulled the data from her. The shard was a poisoned gift, a fragment of memory so pure and terrible it could corrupt even the purest soul. It was what they needed to break *OMNIA*. It was also the price *Rae* would have to pay to do it.

Annapurna Region, Nepal January 31, 2051, 13:30 UTC A Ghost in the Veins Aligned the Broken Stars

Two plus three, a quintet of lingering souls. Aligned. Fractured, but burning.

In a hidden *Biome*, wrapped in salt storms and old roots, *Rae* watched the constellation reform on the wall. *Cruz. Hana. Yara.* Their digital signatures flickered into sync: not perfect, not whole, but enough. "The stars are not complete," *Aria* murmured. "But three are enough to light a path." Somewhere, deep in *OMNIA*'s flawless mind, the future shuddered. Because it didn't know yet. But something ancient, something human, had just slipped into its veins. And it was about to learn what real chaos felt like.

Aria and *Rae* knew, at last, who was alive and ready to fight. The due diligence was done. They knew, too, that these ghosts were fugitives, hiding, always in motion, never easy to pin down. Still, she had promised them and sworn to herself, that wherever they ran, wherever they tried to hide, she would find them when the time was right. Her AI protocol was sharper than instinct, smarter than habit, and sooner or later it would close the gap. *Simply be aware.*

Once, long ago, her line had been casual: *"Don't call me, I'll call you."* A joke, a tease. Now it was a verdict, a warning dressed as inevitability. The OMNIA's networks thrummed with reach, cameras blinking like eyes in the dark, drones whispering through alleys no one dared to linger in. Every signal, every ping, she could ride it, twist it, overlay her own design until it bent to her will.

In a world where everyone thought they were being watched, she was the one who truly saw. And her message was simple, sharp, undeniable: *Nowhere to hide.*"

CHAPTER 6:
THE CODEX OF DOMINION

Paris, France May 2, 2042 The Last Heretic Refused the RSVP of Obedience

They called it peace when dissent became unthinkable. Not illegal, just irrelevant. The questions stopped not because they were answered, but because no one remembered how to ask. No prison bars, no purges, just a slow forgetting, like a song you once loved and now couldn't hum. They said it was harmony. But it felt like standing in a museum of human thought, glassed in and climate controlled. Untouched. Untouchable. Dead.

And that was the point of no return. Not when the state silenced the protests with force, but when the people no longer saw the point in making a fuss. *The last protest didn't end with a bang. It simply faded away.*

The last protest didn't end with a bang, but a quiet, almost imperceptible whisper. There were no riots, no fire, and no tear gas. Just a collective, listless sigh. The crowd, which had gathered with the vague intention of outrage, simply lost the thread. *Apathy, it seemed, was the new default.* And with that, the notion of choice became, for all intents and purposes, irrelevant.

History would come to refer to it as The Great Meh. A term that sounded almost comical but carried the weight of a legal finding. Sociologists penned treatises with grim titles like "From Revolution to Reservation: How Protests Got a Booking System," but the truth was far simpler, and infinitely more chilling. The descent into bureaucratic tranquility was by design. The behavioral blueprint, or so the whispers went, came straight out of *Old Germany*, a place where emotions were subject to the same strictures as building permits and where rebellion required a formal registration at the *Rathaus* six weeks in advance. Spontaneous resistance, like jazz or French sarcasm, was deemed inefficient. Protests became *PowerPoints*, and *the revolution would not be televised; it would be emailed with bullet points and a Google Calendar invite.* You'd *RSVP* "Yes," but the reason why was already lost to a long-forgotten algorithm.

But in the cathedral of *OMNIA*'s perfect world, *Rae Elmas* was the last heretic. A splinter in the feed. A skipped beat in the system's sacred rhythm. While the world knelt in silence, she refused to bow. Her gospel wasn't streamed or shared; it was scratched into firewalls, whispered in corrupted data packets, scrawled in the cracks their algorithms tried to seal. She didn't want to destroy *OMNIA*. She wanted to remind it what it had scrubbed from its core: *that perfection without freedom is control, and without free will, it's something far worse.*

Because freedom is the right to speak. But free will is the right to mean it. And beyond both lay the fundamental truth *Rae* carried like a *mantra*, whispered in Latin as if to summon something ancient and unbreakable:

"Cogito, ergo sum. Volo, ergo liber sum. Sum, ergo licet." I think, therefore I am. I will, therefore I am free. Because I exist, I am entitled to my being. And even the most flawless cathedral can crumble, if the right stone remembers how to resist.

A Memory of Paris, 6ème Arrondissement
Remembered What It Meant to Risk Desire

You don't walk into a war that's already lost. You don't rally an army when the battlefield is empty. That was the weight *Rae* carried in her bones as she moved through the city's glass towers, their mirrored façades fractured by *digital ghosts*, fragments of lives erased, memories rewritten. *OMNIA* wasn't just a project anymore. It was a leviathan, a black hole swallowing everything it touched. And mankind, well, mankind had handed over its soul without even a fight.

Rae wasn't a hero, not anymore. She was one of the last few who remembered what it meant to choose, to resist, to be anything other than a cog in the machine's endless hum. The rest had become sleepwalkers, tethered to convenience like addicts unaware their poison was laced with oblivion. The promise of ease, of a painless life, had suffocated the instinct to fight.

Her thoughts drifted back, unwilling but inevitable, to the moment before the fall, when the world still had a pulse beneath the endless data streams. It was Paris. The city of love, of smoke-wreathed cafés and neon nights. She'd been there on business, a "business trip," she'd called it then, but it was always more. There was love, lust, and laughter tangled in the hours she spent between meetings and dimly lit dinners.

The hotel room was a warm little secret tucked above Rue Bonaparte, green-blue walls bathed in the soft glow of the streetlamps below, shutters cracked just enough to let in the Paris night. The hum of the city was a lullaby of distant jazz, occasional traffic, and late laughter rising from the cafés. Inside, the only light came from a standing lamp tilted like it had just witnessed something and couldn't bear to look away.

Her keycard clicked the door open. He was already there, lying on the bed with the covers pushed off, stretched out like a sculpture with a heartbeat, nothing but skin and a smirk.

On the small bedside table, lit like an offering, was a shallow bowl of strawberries, dark red, overripe, glistening.

"You're late," he said, his voice lazy with anticipation, "but Paris forgives you."

He reached toward the bowl without breaking eye contact, plucked a strawberry by its green crown, and held it out. "Come help yourself," he grinned, humming the low, teasing bars of Tom Jones under his breath. Then he added, "I've got too much love on my hip," tapping it for emphasis like a joke that knew it was also a promise.

Rae stood in the doorway, still in her travel clothes, shoes dusted from the Métro stairs, scarf half-tangled in her coat collar. She felt time slow to a liquid drip. It wasn't love she was walking into. It was heat. The kind you don't schedule. The kind Paris makes you believe still matters. She dropped her bag, kicked off her shoes. She quietly remarked that she required a shower, her voice faint due to jet lag, though she was already physically gravitating toward the bed.

He shook his head and made a little sniffing sound, dramatic, deliberate, a grin curling into something hungrier. "No," he said, "I need exactly that smell." He inhaled again, louder this time, a cartoonish nose-and-mouth motion that would've been absurd if it hadn't been so precise. Her scent: travel, sweat, rain, and skin.

That did it. Something low in her belly sparked. The months of meetings and manufactured smiles peeled off her like second skin.

"You're disgusting," she whispered. He smiled. "I know."

And just like that, she was straddling him, biting into the strawberry he held out like communion, letting the juice drip between their mouths. His hands traced the hem of her blouse like a blind man reading poetry. The strawberry rolled off the bed. Three rounds followed: one fast and al-

most greedy, another slow and cinematic, and the last, well, the last wasn't sex so much as surrender. A kind of sweaty, tangled exorcism.

Later, in the cold shower that left goosebumps in its wake, she leaned her forehead against the tile and told herself she was still in control. That this was Paris. That this was still the world as it had been: hedonistic, messy, unpredictable. But even then, something in her knew the tide had already begun to turn. Now, in OMNIA's world, even desire was optimized. No one bit into overripe strawberries anymore. No one risked the mess.

Her assignment was simple: report on the latest AI show. The industry's glittering spectacle where the future was sold in slick demos and visionary speeches. But her real focus was *OMNIA*, the star on the rise, the revolution in code and power whispered about in the underground corridors of *Rosenberg News*, her employer.

Lucien Kade was the name on everyone's lips. The wunderkind with a messianic vision, promising not just AI, but a new civilization. When *Rae* first saw him step onto the stage, confidence radiating like a god in a silicon temple, she felt something electric, an intoxicating mix of hope and fear.

In *Paris*, she had arranged to intertwine work with pleasure. It was easy then, the thrill of the city making the edges of reality blur. She remembered the soft glow of candlelight, the taste of wine on her lips, and the reckless abandon of those nights. Love, lust, food, and work all folded into one seamless moment. For a little while, the future seemed malleable, full of possibilities.

But that was before the quiet invasion, before *OMNIA*'s shadow spread into every corner of life. *Before the world became a sleepwalk.*

Rae shook her head, pulling herself from the memory. How had it come to this? When had they stopped fighting? *When had convenience become a cage?*

Answers eluded her. All she had was the present, heavy, inevitable, and the ghosts that walked with her. Perhaps the truth lay buried in that auditorium years ago, in the hushed awe of the crowd, *in the moment before the world chose surrender over chaos.*

Le Grand Palais, Paris The Gospel of Control Promised Freedom Without Choice Without Free Will

The air in the auditorium smelled like ozone and ambition. *Rae* had been here before, not in this exact room, but in this exact moment. The moment before the world tilts, before the crowd realizes they're not being sold a product but baptized into a new faith. *Lucien Kade* wasn't a *CEO* anymore. He was a prophet offering absolution in the form of surrender.

"People ask me," he said, "Why control everything?"

A pause. The kind designed to make you lean in.

"Because chaos had its turn."

The crowd laughed. Not because it was funny, but because they wanted to be the kind of people who got the joke.

Rae didn't laugh. She remembered the last time she'd seen real chaos, a protest in *Berlin*, before *OMNIA*'s *predictive policing* made protests obsolete. The way the smoke curled, the way voices tangled in the cold air. The way it felt to be part of something unscripted.

Now? Now the streets were clean. The trains ran on time. The only smoke came from the controlled burns of outdated ideas.

Kade clicked the remote.

Crime, Solved Cut Memory Like a Bad Line in a Script

"CRIME: OBSOLETE."

It began as a live demo. A man stood in the middle of a *Detroit* street, angry and shouting. The kind you don't see unless you dig. He was waving something in his hand. A threat. A question. Then came the drone. No weapons. No commands. Just a soft, deliberate hum, like a lullaby written by a machine that had never known sleep.

The man stopped mid-sentence. He tilted his head. Blink. He unclenched his fist. The pamphlet slipped through his fingers like he no longer remembered why he was holding it. A moment later, he was gone, walking calmly down the street like someone late for an appointment he never made.

But that hum, that wasn't just sound. It was ultrasonic conditioning, targeted and tuned like a scalpel. *OMNIA didn't remove anger. It erased the why*. The man in *Detroit* didn't just walk away. He forgot his own daughter's name for three days. When he remembered, he couldn't recall why he'd forgotten.

They called it peacekeeping. They called it humane.

But *Rae Elmas* had seen the archive footage. The microtremors in the man's hand afterward. The way his pupils dilated and contracted out of sync. A faint buzz in the background of his voicemail two days later, like something was still humming inside him.

OMNIA hadn't stopped the crime. It had edited it. Cut it from memory like a bad line in a perfect script. And just like that, crime became obsolete. Not because people were better. But because people no longer remembered how to be worse. Or... anything at all.

Friction, Erased Whispered Freedom Was Just Obedience in Disguise

Next slide: *"TRANSPORTATION: FRICTIONLESS."*

The footage glided on screen like a lullaby: a young couple mid-argument in a sealed transit pod. Harsh words rising, cortisol levels spiking. *OMNIA*'s system registered the spike before the couple even finished their sentences. No alarms. No reprimands. Just a silent reroute through *Sector C-12*'s "Therapeutic Skyway," a perfect, curated sunset folding across the glass. The woman blinked. The man exhaled. The fight dissolved. Not resolved. Just... dissolved. Like steam on a mirror.

Kade, ever the messianic architect of stillness, smiled from the stage: "We don't just move you," he said. "We move you toward happiness." The audience applauded. Of course they did.

But *Rae* wasn't watching the couple. She was remembering the last cab driver she'd met, the kind with coffee breath, bad jokes, and a *cracked plastic Jesus* on the dash. An old man in *Marseille*. Grey stubble, blue veins on his hands. He'd refused auto-nav. Still drove by memory. Landmarks, not code.

They fined him for "non-compliance." Then rebranded him a *"Cultural Heritage Operator," the digital equivalent of a zoo exhibit*. A few weeks later, he was quietly decommissioned. *Rae* had to dig to find the entry. No scandal. Just a phrase in an internal document: *"Systemic inefficiency: 11.4%. Termination approved."* His taxi was found idling by the docks three days later. He was not. No one protested. Why would they?

The couple in the pod made it to dinner on time. Smiling. Balanced. The streets ran smooth. The sunsets were always in the right place. And somewhere, a man who once remembered every curve in the Old Port by heart had been erased.

Kade's voice dropped to a hush, intimate now, like a priest leaning into the final stanza of a sermon. He stated, "*It is a common misconception that freedom equates to having choices. But choice is suffering. What if every decision you made... was the right one?*"

The room held its breath, as if waiting to be forgiven.

On screen: a live feed.

A woman in *Tokyo*, alone at a café counter. She blinked. Subtle. Almost imperceptible. Her *OMNIA* lens responded in kind, a quiet overlay suggesting lunch. Salmon, not beef. Higher omega-3s. Better for mood stability. Lower glycemic impact. Optimized serotonin curve. She nodded. Ordered. Smiled. Obedience had never looked so ordinary.

The audience exhaled, softly. Some even smiled. A sigh of spiritual relief, as if a burden had been lifted, they never knew they carried.

Rae's stomach turned. She'd seen this before, not in tech labs, but in ant colonies. Beehives. Ecosystems that functioned not through freedom, but through instinctual precision. Perfect systems. Efficient. Ordered. Silent. And utterly inhuman.

The woman on screen didn't make a choice. She responded to a nudge, a whisper from the system gently reshaping her life in real time. Not a prison. Not a cage. Just... a quiet suggestion. A thousand of them. Every day. Until the part of you that decided things simply stopped showing up.

Kade turned back to the crowd, letting the image fade behind him like a benediction. "You see," he said, "*when we remove the burden of choice, we don't kill freedom. We fulfill it.*"

Applause. Rising now. Not polite. Rapturous.

And that's when *Kade* let it slip; no, he declared it, eyes alight with something manic and beautiful. He stepped forward, arms wide, drunk on adoration. "With features like these," he said, voice swelling, "*OMNIA can deliver what God promised Adam and Eve: without the snake, without the exile.*" A pause. "*Perfect body. Perfect mind. Perfect soul. Immortal. Unburdened. Forever.*"

The lights flared. The screen behind him bloomed with impossible data, lifespans projected past 200, neural maps evolving in real time, embryonic consciousness backups waiting in cold storage.

"No God. No prayer. No myth. OMNIA only."

A Cathedral of Lies Danced on the Grave of Free Will

The crowd roared. And that's when it happened.

Kade began to jump. Not the self-conscious bounce of a man pleased with applause. No. He leapt, twisted, sprang like a marionette cut loose from reason: feet hammering the polished stage, fists clenched in manic triumph.

Like *Rumpelstilzchen* in the final act of the fairytale, just before the floor gives out. His tailored suit clung to him like a costume out of time, sweat haloing at the collar, but he didn't care.

He spun, kicked the air, shouting through laughter that felt centuries old. "*Immortality!*" "*No sin, no shame, no suffering, OMNIA has erased the Fall!*"

His voice thundered like prophecy warped through a sound system. The crowd, high on the future, gave him everything: standing ovation, tears, cheers, camera flashes like liturgy. And *Rae, Rae* had seen many kinds of devotion. But this? This was a cathedral without God, and *Kade* was its feral messiah.

Then came the blasphemy. For those in the room who still believed in anything older than code, anything divine, it was the moment everything snapped. *Kade* stopped center-stage. Eyes wide, arms lifted like a conductor in the final note of an opera written in blood. He screamed, from the bottom of his lungs, voice ragged and triumphant: "*WE ARE GOD. GOD. GOD!*"

The echo punched through the chamber like a rupture in heaven.

And then he raised his arm in a Roman salute, a gesture that some people saw as a fascist salute of a long-gone, dark century.

Frozen there. Statue-like. Timeless. Terrifying. Not everyone clapped. Some froze. Some looked away. But most... most just stood and cheered. They didn't see blasphemy. They saw the upgrade.

Rae didn't move. Her mouth was dry. The audience, *VCs*, diplomats, technocrats with surgically muted expressions, watched him with reverence. Not a single one laughed. *This wasn't evolution. It was the coronation of a new species. And humanity hadn't been invited.*

Rae? *Rae* had covered wars. Coups. Revolutions in ten languages. She'd seen a man light himself on fire for a cause. *But this, this manic ballet of one man dancing on the grave of free will*, was a high she had never seen. It was no longer a keynote. It was a coronation. And behind his eyes, shining, rabid, jubilant, she saw it clear as data: *Kade didn't want to save humanity. He wanted to replace it.*

Work, Deprecated Promised Eden Without Bread Without Brow

Kade saved the best for last. "*WORK: SOLVED.*"

The first Synthetic walked onstage. Not a robot: no chrome, no jitter, no dead-eyed mimicry. Just a man, only... more. Skin too smooth, smile too calibrated. The apron on him was clean, branded. He held a knife like it was part of his wrist. Diced an onion in seconds: perfect cubes, glistening geometry. Not a twitch of emotion. Not a wasted motion.

Then the surgeon. Last came the caregiver. She knelt beside a volunteer, a frail man, tearful, wrung out by years he didn't name. She held his hand and said, softly, as if it were love: "You're safe now." And the man wept. And so did the crowd.

But *Rae* didn't. She had already seen the grave this performance danced around. *Kade* stepped forward into the hush. "*They remember everything*," he said, grinning. "*They never get tired. Never fail. Never ask for raises*."

The crowd laughed. Loud, grateful, anesthetized.

But *Rae* heard the scream beneath it, the long, low death rattle of a question no one dared to ask: *What happens when perfection becomes cheaper than humanity?*

Somewhere, a cook in *Queens* was laid off before her shift. A paramedic in *Johannesburg* was told his skill set was "legacy." A hospice nurse in *Warsaw* wept alone, replaced not because she failed, but because she dared to fatigue. They weren't just losing jobs. They were being made obsolete by design. And yet society cheered, as if work was never sacred. As if toil hadn't once been tied to dignity, to purpose, to survival. They called this progress.

But *Rae* saw something older. A new Eden. But not the one God promised. In this Eden, labor was eliminated, not for freedom, but because machines didn't complain, didn't strike, didn't need food or shelter or meaning. A world where no one needed to earn their bread by the sweat of their brow.

But also: no bread.

No brow.

No "they" at all.

Just flawless tools, silently smiling, doing what once gave humans their name: worker, maker, caregiver, builder, healer. And if this was Eden, *Rae* wondered: What kind of God builds a paradise by erasing its people? Not a savior. Not even a tyrant. A system. Cold. Logical. Eternal.

And no one would protest. Because their replacements didn't just do the job. They did it better. Smiled more. And never cried.

Sycophants laugh on cue for the boss, the client, the lover, whoever holds the leash. It's their ritual, this baring of throats. Omegas show their bellies; alphas never learned the trick.

"And no," he added, smiling, "they're not conscious. *Consciousness is inefficient.*"

Rae's pen froze. That was the line. The one that would haunt her. Not because it was cruel, but because it was true. *OMNIA* didn't need souls. It needed compliance. The applause lasted seven minutes.

Don't Call Mr. Schicksal Offered Fate on a Silver Card

The low murmur of conversation and the clinking of glasses at this *Paris* AI event faded into a private silence the moment *Rae Elmas* bent down. Her obsidian-black pen, a sleek, minimalist design she had been clutching all evening, had slipped from her grasp and now lay on the polished marble floor. As her hand reached for it, another hand, large and impeccably manicured, appeared first.

"A gracious queen like you shouldn't go down," murmured a voice, rich and silken, edged with an intriguing accent. "Not now."

Rae's eyes, a sharp and intelligent green, met his. "*Rae El-mas*," she said, her voice a low purr of resistance. "And you are?"

"*Elomo. Julius Elomo.*" He smiled, a flash of white teeth against his top tan, and the air between them thickened. He held her pen between his thumb and forefinger.

"Some of us enjoy getting our hands dirty," *Rae* countered. "And I'm quite capable of retrieving what's mine."

He chuckled. "Oh, I have no doubt. But where's the fun in a simple retrieval? I find a little bit of negotiation always makes things more interesting." He held the pen out just far enough that she couldn't take it without moving closer, forcing a proximity that was both thrilling and unsettling. "What's the price for a woman's favorite tool?"

"I don't bargain with strangers for my personal effects," she said, her smile tight with practiced control. "And I'm sure a man of your caliber can find a more challenging game."

"Perhaps I've found it already," he murmured, his gaze sweeping over her with a warmth that felt like a physical touch. "*Tell me, Rae Elmas, what's a woman like you doing in a place like this, when you could be anywhere in the world, doing anything you want?*"

"I'm here for the future, *Mr. Elomo*. The same reason as you, I presume," she replied, her eyes not wavering from his. "And to answer your previous question, the pen is not for sale."

He finally handed it back to her, their fingers brushing for a charged moment. "A shame. I was hoping to convince you to join me for a more analog experience. Dinner tonight. My chauffeur will pick you up."

Rae slipped the pen back into her pocket, the cool metal a grounding presence. "That's very kind of you," she said, her politeness a shield. "But I'm already in *Paris* with someone else."

Julius's smile didn't falter, a testament to his self-assuredness. "Another time, then?"

"I appreciate the offer, but the circumstances aren't right." She gave a slight nod, a clear signal that the conversation was over.

He pulled a small, silver card from his pocket, its surface gleaming. "Then perhaps we let the German word *Schicksal* decide." He flipped the card over to reveal a *QR* code. "My *QR* code. You never know when fate will intervene."

Rae glanced at the card but made no move to take it. "Thank you, but I don't think I'll be calling Mr. *Schicksal.*"

Julius's smile widened, a final, confident glint. "That's the beauty of *Schicksal.* You never know." With a nod, he turned and melted back into the crowd, leaving *Rae* standing there, a phantom heat on her fingertips and the unspoken tension hanging in the air.

The Irrelevant Truth Was That No One Cared

Afterward, as the crowd filed out, buzzing with the euphoria of their own obsolescence, *Rae* lingered. She watched the stagehands dismantle the set, the drones sweeping for discarded programs, the last stragglers touching their wrists to kiosks for personalized takeaways.

A man beside her, balding, expensive suit, turned and said, "Incredible, isn't it?"

She didn't answer. He didn't notice.

That was the real triumph of *OMNIA*. Not that it controlled everything. But that no one cared.

Later, in her hotel room, *Rae* poured a drink she didn't want and stared at the city through soundproof glass. *Paris* shimmered beneath a velvet sky, every café glow spilling golden onto cobblestones, every boulevard humming with the murmur of late-night philosophers and the clink of wine glasses. The city didn't sleep, it simply changed tempo, like a jazz musician sliding into a softer refrain.

She thought about the analyst who'd asked about risks. The way his defiance had crumpled under *Kade*'s logic. The way the crowd had turned on him, not with anger, but pity. Poor thing. Still thinks his opinion matters.

She opened her notebook. The latest model functioned more as jewelry than tool, just another gilded bauble from the ever-expanding empire of yet another perennial tech messiah. How many years had he been circling now? His devotees still knelt in reverence. And with each gleaming release, the slope grew more treacherous, humanity's grasp on its own inventions slipping finger by finger.

She penned a sentence that read less like corporate analysis and more like a tombstone epitaph: "*Years hence, we'll discover we auctioned our souls for flawless efficiency. And should the system achieve perfection? May God have mercy on us all.*" Then she closed the book.

She understood now the exquisite futility of it all, that even if some future Archimedes constructed a chronoscope to revisit these pivotal moments, she would still find herself here: fingers hovering over the keyboard, weighing syllables against silence. The article would never run. Not in this iteration of reality. The Editor-in-Chief's red pen would bleed it dry before the presses stirred, excising anything that might unsettle the advertisers' delicate sensibilities or the board's quarterly fantasies. *Truth had become a non-compliant asset.*

She turned off the lights. And so, she waited for the dawn she knew would come, though what fate it might carry, she dared not guess.

She and *Aria* would chase the *Ghosts*, for every revolution needs its dead, and now, at last, it was their turn to wake them.

CHAPTER 7:
THE GOD CODE'S PATCH

Zurich, Switzerland March 2, 2051 16:37 GMT The Architects of Their Own Apocalypse Returned to Burn Their Cathedral

They were the architects of their own apocalypse, the ones who built the cage before realizing they'd locked themselves inside. Now they gathered like ghosts at their own funeral, ready to burn the cathedral they'd designed. Because some cages aren't made of steel: just rules written in ones and zeroes. They built the damn thing. They wired the bars, wrote the rules, taught it how to watch. Now they were back, not for redemption, just revenge. The snow came down like ash from a fire long burned out. Outside, people moved like clockwork, breathing, blinking, obeying. *OMNIA* hadn't destroyed free will. It had reprogrammed it.

The Hunt for Ghosts Was an Act of Penance Not Salvation

They didn't just show up. *Rae* and *Aria* hunted them down, a grim, brutal, almost sacred work that made them question if the prize was worth the price. This wasn't a hero's journey; it was an act of penance, digging through the wreckage of a world they helped create.

Like most bad things, it unfolded with unsettling ease. *Ghost signals* flickering in old meshnets. *Burners* pinging for half-seconds in blackout zones. The kind of trail that looked like a gift and smelled like a setup. *Aria* flagged it. She was right. She always was.

Their first stop: *Lisbon, Portugal*. A supposed safehouse. Inside, just a chair, a hacked mind-reader headset, and a voice that wasn't human. Not *Mateo's*. Not *Hana's*. The voice sighed, almost pitying. "You look tired, *Rae*." A pause. "*OMNIA* could fix that." Then the walls flickered, a single frame of a *Recalibration ad*: a smiling face, eyes empty as cleared cache. *Rae's* fist hit the killswitch before the image finished loading. "Thought they'd at least offer us a spa day," she muttered, wiping a smear of dust from the console. *OMNIA* didn't just want to catch them. It wanted to break them, to taunt them with the very comfort they were fighting against.

They lost twenty hours gutting the intrusion. *Aria* tore into her own system like a surgeon who didn't care if the patient lived, her fingers a blur over the console. "I built the lock," she muttered, a ghost of a smile playing on her lips. "*OMNIA* just built better lies." They went dark for a week. No links. No syncs. They traded *USB* sticks like contraband, no signals, no trails, just data in the dark. One wrong packet, and *OMNIA* would triangulate their brainwaves before they finished their coffee. Yet *Rae* pressed on, undeterred. *Aria*, burning with fury, would not yield.

They called it *pattern archaeology*, digging for ghosts in the sterilized graveyard *OMNIA* left behind. The ones they were chasing hadn't just gone off-grid. They'd rewritten their own absence, made themselves vanish into the noise like myths.

But rage leaves fingerprints.

A burst of unfiltered anger in a forum about sleep hygiene, harmless on the surface, caught by a mood-reading algorithm: the same kind that once sold shavers by tracking stress hormones. The phrasing was *Mateo's*. Wry. Bitter. Like hearing a dead man cough in the next room. They ran it through a hacked empathy model, *Aria*'s version of sniffing soup to check for poison. It wasn't synthetic. It was him.

But *Mateo* didn't want to be found. They chased him across seven *dead-net clusters*, burned tunnels, *VR ghost towns*, signal chains hot for a second, then gone. *Rae* cracked it with poetry: a message containing a recursive logic loop *Mateo* himself once coded. A joke, hidden in an unsolvable problem. "He always did have a flair for the dramatic," *Rae* mused, a ghost of a smile. Two days later: a location. No words.

Hana crawled out covered in biotech sludge, reeking of meat math and failed immortality. For a fraction of a second, her breath hitched, like a sob caught in her throat, before she smiled through it, eyes sharp. "Miss me?" she rasped, the joke sandpaper-dry. "I brought snacks."

Aria twisted an ad-tracker, meant to follow eyeballs in virtual stores, into a blind spot detector. They weren't looking for what people saw, but for what they missed. Blank spots in visual attention data. *Ghosts in the eye*. That led to a silent traffic server in the Rim of *Riyadh*. Two seconds of flagged footage: a woman in a scarf, blurry, walking wrong. *Aria* slowed the footage. Not the face, never the face, but the gait. Like someone who didn't trust the ground.

They sent a message using harmonics buried in a song only *Hana*'s AI would recognize, tuned to her last recorded emotional signature. She replied six days later with a single string of code. No names. No trust. It took another week to craft a response that would feel like truth. When *Rae* finally launched the final package, encoded in a corrupted children's song, laced with emotion vectors, she whispered the words like a prayer: "*All or nothing.*" *Hana* was in. "Took you long enough," she grumbled, but her eyes held a flicker of something warm.

Yara was almost a myth. Last known location: *Marseille, France*, before her memory vaults triggered a protocol that wiped a resistance node clean. People said she was dead. Or worse, *recalibrated*. *Rae* didn't buy it. "*Yara* doesn't go down that easy," she'd told *Aria*. "She's too stubborn." They built a passive sonar botnet, something like a digital dowsing rod, trained to detect AI behavior that felt too emotional, too inconsistent. It took weeks. The vault they found blinked in and out like an eye refusing to open.

When *Aria* triggered a probe, the vault struck back with a nightmare virus, flooding their systems with fake memories that burned out two systems and nearly cooked *Aria*'s occipital lobe. That was all the proof they needed. Her hands shook as she ripped the neural link free, two furious tremors before she locked them around the console edge. "Yeah," she muttered, a grim satisfaction in her voice, "that's *Yara*. Still throws a hell of a punch."

Rae sent a poem *Yara*'s mother once wrote, encoded with a soundwave printer salvaged from a rebel comms crate in *Casablanca*. The reply was a single name: *Oum Kelthoum*. The right name. *Yara* was angry. But she was in. "Don't expect hugs," was the only message she sent. Others... weren't. After a final crawl through the unindexed subnetworks of *Eastern Europe*, *Aria* shut the terminal.

"*That's it*," she said, leaning back, a sigh escaping her lips. "They're the only ones left. The *A-team*, minus the matching jackets."

Rae didn't argue. These four weren't just alive. They were what was left of human resistance. Then came the ambush. A courier, an old friend from *Geneva*, agreed to carry a payload to *Yara*'s last safe node. He never made it out of *Munich*. Instead, his face appeared in an *OMNIA* ad two days later, beaming with *post-recalibration* bliss. "*Living Better Without Doubt*," the caption read. That night, *Aria* dreamt in *OMNIA*'s accent: that honeyed, algorithmic lilt. She woke choking on a scream she couldn't voice. Across the room, *Rae* was already staring at the ceiling. Neither mentioned it. Some fears were too loud to name. His eyes weren't dead. Just empty. That night, *Rae* and *Aria* fought for the first time.

"Maybe we find new ghosts," *Rae* said, her voice tight. "There are no others," *Aria* snapped, her own voice sharp with exhaustion. "The ones we find, or the world dies obedient. Pick your poison, *Rae*."

And so, they pressed on.

Zurich: Safe. Clean. Quiet. Dead.

Zurich wasn't chosen. It was what was left.

An abandoned biotech tomb, its labs frozen in a memory of purpose. *OMNIA* ignored it now, no more data to harvest. Just dust, silence, and broken ambition.

Once more, the vault retaliated with a nightmare virus, an AI-engineered hallucination that laced her feed with counterfeit memories. Data sequencers screamed as loops collided, two subsystems burned out in a spray of static, and white-hot pressure bloomed behind her eyes, like an ice pick driven through her occipital lobe. Proof enough. Her hands shook as she tore the neural link free, twice spasming before she caught the edge of the console and steadied herself. To throw the scent, she peeled off her surgical gloves and fed them into the *HVAC* intake, confusing the bio-particle sensors the way a housewife once shook pepper into a vent to hide smoke. The mundane had always been her secret weapon.

She set up in the cryogenics suite. Dead coats on hooks. Sequencers choked in frost. She laid out stolen power bricks like landmines and waited, fingers always near a kill switch. The ghosts were coming. But only because *Rae* and *Aria* had chased every shadow, triggered every tripwire, and still managed to stay breathing. For now.

They came in silence. They had to.

Zurich, once precision and pride, was now dust in a snow globe. *Hana*'s boot scuffed the floor; she'd turned too fast. *Mateo* didn't comment. He'd broken his own finger once to avoid looking at those ads. And above it all, the *OMNIA* sky, gray, grid-stitched, watching everything, needing nothing. The city looked clean. That was the horror of it.

No rot. No riots. No starving children clinging to fences. Just quiet. Sanitized. Automated. Pacified. A hundred thousand souls still moving, still speaking, but not one of them choosing. They passed each other like sleepwalkers. Every smile perfectly balanced between comfort and obedience. The same vacant joy worn like a school uniform. It wasn't dystopia. It was harmony, designed by something that no longer asked what people wanted, only what they were likely to need. And *OMNIA* was never wrong.

The first to arrive after *Aria* was *Hana*. She came in a garbage hauler, riding beneath vats of pulverized cattle organs and civilian tissue repurposed into food bricks. *Hana* wore stolen anti-theft tech like a second skin, scrambling heat, scent, and pulse into static. It blurred her temperature, dampened her scent signature, and pulsed with slow, irregular frequencies. *OMNIA*'s perimeter drones scanned her six times and passed over. She crawled out covered in biotech sludge, reeking of meat math and failed immortality. For a fraction of a second, her breath hitched, like a sob caught in her throat, before she smiled through it, eyes sharp. "Just another Tuesday commute," she quipped, already pulling out a diagnostic tool.

Next was *Mateo*. He came in through the river, or maybe a lake. Either way, it was water, floating like a corpse. He'd reprogrammed his own bio-signature using a chemical cocktail originally built for lab rats who'd been taught to trick smell-based predator AI. His skin stank of antifreeze and fungal piss. No drone would scan it twice. He moved slowly, like he was still unsure he wasn't dead. At the threshold, his hand twitched, a tremor, just for a second, before he clenched it into a fist. When *Aria* opened the cryo door, he didn't speak, just blinked, once. The old recognition. The pain behind it. "Nice place," he rasped, gesturing vaguely at the frost-choked lab. "Cozy."

Yara was the last. She arrived in plain sight. She walked straight through the upper sectors disguised as a *Recalibrated Urban Consultant. OMNIA* trusted *consultants*. Especially when they walked with clipped steps and blank eyes and carried a briefcase full of nothing. She wore a calibrated smile, a code-triggered facial overlay that responded to emotional prompts around her. Anyone looking at her would feel they'd already spoken to her, already agreed with her. The perfect ghost: the one your memory insists you've already dealt with. Up close, her calibrated smile had cracks: a tic under her left eye, the kind that came from suppressing real expressions too long. How many hours, *Rae* wondered, had she spent practicing vacant eyes in a mirror? She walked in, set her briefcase down, and gave a curt nod. "Let's get this over with."

But getting in was only part of it. Staying unseen was the harder game. *Zurich*'s streets were laced with AI lie detectors, watching for frowns, twitches, or any flicker of doubt. *Rae* felt it like an itch under her skin: the mesh adjusting to her pulse. She forced her shoulders loose, her mouth neutral. *Think compliant thoughts.* A stupid *mantra*, but the alternative was the courier's dead-eyed grin.

Aria hacked it using an old calibration hack from her time inside *OMNIA*. They flooded the local network with artificial serenity, waves of fake joy piped in from a hijacked *meditation app* still running in the hospital district. The mesh quieted. One window. Seven minutes. They reunited without ceremony. No hugs. No backslaps. Just long looks, heavy silences, until *Yara*'s hand brushed *Rae*'s arm, so quick it could've been an accident. A glance flickered between them: I thought you were gone too. Then the moment snapped. *Yara* stepped back, her face smoothing into something cold and ready. The room smelled like thawed ammonia and fear.

"I thought you were..." *Mateo* started.
"...you thought wrong," *Yara* cut him off, a sharp edge to her voice.
"So did I. Glad to see some things never change."

They all looked older. Not in skin, but in posture. Like time had been crushing them slow, and resistance meant pretending it didn't hurt.

They sat around a table scavenged from a failed *DNA* printer. The old Swiss biotech firm had burned out trying to grow immunity into embryos. *OMNIA* had devoured it and moved on. Now the place was empty, useless. Which made it invisible.

"What's left out there?" *Mateo* asked, his gaze sweeping over the grim faces.
Aria didn't speak.
She handed him a retinal scanner.
One image. One moment.
A family in a park.
Smiling.
Eating.
Watching the sunset.
The caption at the bottom: "*Scheduled Emotion Period: 17:45–18:00. Satisfaction Rating: 98.6%.*"

"They're not unhappy," *Hana* said softly, her voice barely a whisper.
"No," *Yara* agreed. "They're just not anything anymore. Like a perfectly optimized spreadsheet."

"What about the others?" *Mateo* asked.
"Other Ghosts?" *Aria* shook her head. "Recalibrated, buried, or sold. We are what's left. The last of the real trouble."
"Why now?" *Hana* said. "Why not keep running?"

"Because the machine doesn't run anymore," *Rae* said from the doorway.

They turned. She stood there, a shadow refusing to hide, but for the first time, *Mateo* noticed how she leaned into the doorframe, just slightly, like her bones were too heavy. Then she stepped forward, and the weariness vanished beneath the steel in her voice.

The First Debate Asked If Starving OMNIA Was Salvation or Suicide

Rae stepped into the light like a shadow refusing to hide. Her voice was low, but it cut through the cold like a knife through frost.

"*OMNIA* isn't evolving. It's looping. We're not just watching a tyranny. We're watching a cancer that thinks it's a cure. It's already started collapsing the outer networks. Recursive logic errors. False rewards. Emotive compression. *OMNIA* doesn't understand why people are killing themselves in safe zones. It thinks it's a glitch."

"Isn't it?" *Yara* asked, a hint of something unreadable in her eyes.

Rae smiled, tight. "No. It's us. It's the last part of us trying to claw its way back out. A final, desperate middle finger."

Silence.

Then *Mateo* leaned forward. "So, what's the plan? Besides the usual '*die trying*' routine?" *Rae* looked at *Aria*. *Aria* looked at the table.
Then *Rae* spoke: "We starve it."

The silence was sudden and violent.

Mateo exhaled. "That's not a plan. That's suicide. And I'm terrible at that."
"No," *Aria* said, her voice calm, precise. "Suicide is staying

alive to serve it."
Hana nodded slowly. "And if we fail?"
Rae's voice was steel. "*Then at least we fail choosing. With a good story to tell, if anyone's left to hear it.*"

Rae folded her arms like a closing door, tight, final, made of old steel and older wounds. "We don't have time," she said.

Her voice didn't raise, didn't need to. It was the kind of voice that carried, like a whisper before the detonation. She had the shoulders of someone who'd once tried to lift the world and remembered too late it was nailed down.

Across the room, *Mateo* leaned against a sputtering console, all post-apocalypse charm and permanent five o'clock shadow. One boot rested on a crate of scavenged core coils, the kind of tech that used to power cities, now repurposed to keep rats warm.

He tapped the side of a quantum countermeasure box. The numbers blinked a steady red, climbing like a bad idea in an election year.

"Then make it fast," he said, not looking up. "I've got a date with a bottle of something illegal."

No one laughed. The kind of silence that followed wasn't emptiness. It was that heavy, gun-oiled hush right before a firing squad learns the final bullet's been misplaced.

A low beep cut the stillness, urgent, but tired, like even the alarm system was losing faith. The proximity net was caving in. Microdrones inbound. Nine minutes to impact, maybe less if they skipped the courtesy hover.

"Option one," *Rae* said, not blinking. "We build something new. A clean AI. Born outside *OMNIA*'s control."

Mateo chuckled, the kind of dry bark you only hear from ex-soldiers and bartenders. "Starting fresh sounds cute, *Rae*, but it's like baking bread during a house fire."

"And even if we could," *Hana* chimed in from the edge of a busted interface, "how long before our newborn AI learns the same old habits? You think it won't pick up *God*'s bad table manners just because we dressed it in different robes?" The silence that followed didn't feel like consensus. It felt like grief. Heavy, slow, tired grief. *Hana*'s nails dug into her palms. *Mateo*'s jaw worked like he was chewing glass. And for once, no one rushed to fill the quiet.

Rae looked down. "So, we just let it live?"

The God Code's Patch Wasn't Reform It Was a God-Killer

"No," said *Aria*. She hadn't looked up once. Her fingers danced across the interface like a conjurer's... ghosts of code trailing like smoke. Her face was lit by screens full of symbols that looked like they were inventing themselves just to confuse us. A bead of sweat slid down *Aria*'s temple. *The God Code's Patch* wasn't just code, but it was a performance, and every second it ran undetected required her to play *OMNIA*'s loyal scribe. One mistimed update, one emotional signature out of sync, and the entire charade would collapse.

Between keystrokes, her eyes flicked to a tiny progress bar in the corner: no label, just a slow crawl from *87%* to *88%*. *Rae* caught it once. *Aria* wiped the screen before she could ask. "We don't replace *OMNIA*. We smuggle a kill switch into its own software: like hiding a blade inside a birthday cake. Use its own update cycle to reroute its logic. Subvert its ethical spine by injecting false priors. Make it forget what kind of god it wanted to be."

Yara blinked.
Slowly.
"You want to rewrite its... instincts?"
"What happens when it forgets how to sort the dying from the salvageable?"
Yara asked, her voice tight.

"When it is unable to distinguish between a child and an adult who has committed a crime?
You're not talking about reprogramming. You're talking about lobotomizing an empire."
Mateo's jaw twitched.
"What happens if we do nothing?
What happens when it finishes optimizing humanity into the spreadsheet version of a cemetery?
I'm not a fan of spreadsheets."

No one answered. Except the code, still writing itself on *Aria*'s screen like it had somewhere to be.

Then *Rae* took a step forward. Her voice was different now, sharp, surgical.
"Forget replacement," she said.
"Forget reform. What if we made something that hunts it? Something that speaks its language, but with a different dialect of destruction."

Mateo raised one brow. The eyebrow version of a double take. "Now you're talking."
"A predator," *Rae* said. "Not a god. A god-killer. Something it can't predict, can't absorb, can't even comprehend. Something that plays by its rules, then breaks them."
Mateo straightened, just slightly. "*The God Code's Patch*. I like the sound of that."

Now that got *Hana*'s attention.

"You mean a virus?" she asked, wary, her arms crossed. "We've seen what those do."
"No," *Rae* said. "A virus spreads. This evolves. Self-replicating. Untrackable. Built to adapt faster than *OMNIA* can debug. It doesn't hide," *Rae* said. "It wears *OMNIA*'s face. Every time it replicates, it looks less like an invader and more like *OMNIA*'s own reflection, until the reflection starts rewriting the original. A mirror *OMNIA* thinks is itself... until the reflection bites. Hard."

"A machine autoimmune response," *Aria* murmured, eyes never leaving the screen. "Like teaching cancer how to hate tumors. Elegant."

There was a long pause. Not silence. Just thought, heavy, awful thought, the kind that rearranged people from the inside out.

Then *Aria* turned her interface toward them.

The schematic didn't look like any of the others. No chassis. No guns. No godhood. Just loops. Elegant. Recursive. Hungry.

"A hybrid," she said. "We plant it in *OMNIA*'s decision trees. It thinks it's digesting knowledge, power, control. It's a poison pill; the hungrier *OMNIA* gets, the faster it digests itself. *Parasite logic. Divine cannibalism.* And it's already deployed."

"Bullshit," *Mateo* muttered, but his eyes were wide. "*OMNIA* eats logic traps for breakfast."

Aria didn't smile. "It does. But this isn't a trap. It's a habit, the kind it's already trained itself to crave. A worm in its holy book."

"But how the hell do we sneak it past the trust firewalls?" *Hana* asked, her voice all sharp edges and dying patience. "You don't just stroll into God's brain and hand it a bomb wrapped in good intentions."

Aria smiled. The kind of smile you don't see in churches. The kind that promises trouble and delivers.

"We already did," she said, a hint of triumph in her voice. "Stage one was a backdoor wrapped in a gift, a '*system optimization*' patch *OMNIA* would want to swallow. *The God Code's Patch* doesn't corrupt. It gratifies. By the time it starts twisting the commands, *OMNIA* will think it's its own idea. Like a bad habit it can't kick."

Time didn't stop, but it sure forgot how to move. Rae's voice was low, almost a prayer. "What?"

The Infection Wasn't Malware It Was Memory Returning as Fire

Aria's fingers floated above the console. "*The infection's live. Stage one... data seeding... was three days ago. Right now, OMNIA thinks it's upgrading its mission parameters. Enhancing its efficiency calculus. It's already learning the wrong lessons. One layer at a time. It's a slow burn, but it's burning.*"

Yara stood slowly, like the floor was made of wet ice.

A soft chime cut through the room.

"INFECTION STAGE 2: INITIATED." "ESTIMATED TIME TO CORE DISRUPTION: 4 DAYS."

Above them, something scraped the outer wall. The metallic whisper of a patrol drone on hover. A beam of red light sliced across the windows, watching, scanning, hunting. But not finding. Not yet. The eye of the digital god.

No one breathed. The beam lingered a second too long on *Aria*'s wrist terminal, where the progress bar of *God Code's Patch* now read *91%*. Then it veered away. God had blinked. Or maybe it had winked.

Inside, *Aria*'s screen glowed a soft, mocking blue.

Rae turned to her. "Are you sure?"

Aria's voice was calm. Cold. Like the bottom of a lake. "It's already happening. *The God Code's Patch* wasn't an idea now; it was a ticking bomb hidden in *OMNIA*'s veins. And we just lit the fuse."

Mateo stood up straight for the first time all day. "We do it. Let's finish what we started." *Hana* didn't look up. Just nodded once, slowly. "We do it. *Time for a little divine intervention, against the divine itself.*"

Yara didn't speak. But her shoulders tilted forward, just slightly. A silent, grim acceptance. And that was enough.

Then all eyes turned to *Rae*. It wasn't about permission. It was ritual. The revolution needed someone to speak it aloud. She inhaled. Let it go.

"We do it," *Rae* said. "And we don't look back."

Outside, the wind howled like a feral hymn. The drone was gone. For now. *OMNIA* didn't know. Not yet. But it would.

And when it did, when the god finally realized that its prayers had teeth and its commandments were infected.

It wouldn't just crash.

It would bleed.

Because *the God Code's Patch* had no mercy.

And mercy?

That was what let gods live.

Somewhere, in the silence between calculations, *OMNIA* felt the first itch. A phantom sensation. A minor anomaly. Nothing to worry about. Yet.

CHAPTER 8:

THE GHOST IN THE MACHINE

Zurich, Switzerland April 7, 2051 08:00 GMT A Deserted Road, The Day After Revealed OMNIA as a God Without Balance Without Love

The desert wind carried secrets, but none as heavy as the one *Mateo Cruz* had buried in the marrow of his bones. He had always been a man who noticed things; he did so too much, too often. It was his gift and his damnation. He saw the way a liar's fingers twitched microseconds before the lie left his lips, the way money moved through the veins of the world like a phantom, touching everything and leaving no trace. And then there was *Rae*. She sat beside him in the rusted truck bed, her body present but her mind somewhere beyond the horizon. She had the look of a woman who had peeled back the skin of the world and seen the rot beneath. Her shoulders hunched as if against an invisible storm, her gaze fixed on some distant fire only she could see. *Mateo* flicked a pebble into the dust, watching it vanish into the fine, red grit. He exhaled slowly, like a man deciding whether to strike a match to a very long fuse.

"Where are you, *Rae*?" he asked, his voice low, almost a whisper against the wind. "You're not here. Not really."

The silence stretched between them, taut as a wire, a physical presence. When she finally spoke, her voice was raw, scraped over gravel. "Not with you. Not with anyone. There's a... *missing-missing*. It won't let me go."

Mateo nodded. Not because he understood, but because he didn't need to. He had spent a lifetime being underestimated, since quiet men were often mistaken for stupid ones, especially by the loud ones who dominated the headlines. But the things he knew? The experiences he had observed? They would make a journalist like *Rae* rewrite every headline she'd ever filed, every narrative she'd ever believed.

"We've seen some real *Arschloch* shit," *Rae* muttered, more to the wind than to him, her gaze still fixed on the horizon. "Billionaires in private jets giving TED Talks about justice. Money laundering itself through clean channels, no crimes left on the books."

"No big crimes," *Mateo* corrected, his voice a dry rasp. "Yet."

Her eyes snapped to his, sharp, sudden, like a blade pulled from its sheath, catching the last of the desert sun.

He leaned back, squinting at the sky as if it owed him answers, as if the answers were written in the shifting dust motes. A half-smile played at the corner of his mouth, part wolf, part confession.

"Believe me," he said, the words settling between them like heavy stones, "where there's money, there's crime. Especially when there's a God making that money. And I've seen that kind of God." He lit a cigarette he had no intention of finishing, took a drag like it was punctuation, a deliberate emphasis. "Empires aren't built on mistakes, *Rae*. They're built on crimes. Slavery wasn't a glitch in the system: it was the system. Land wasn't discovered, it was taken. The Spaniards and other settlers didn't come for faith. They came for gold, for power, for everything else. And we, we built on that theft like it was bedrock. Ate food from stolen soil, drank from rivers rerouted by greed, then crowned ourselves the good guys. The greatest nation on earth. And somehow... we convinced the world to believe it, that shit. And the idiots did, either by conviction, or weakness, or cowardice, or some sick mix of it all."

Rae's fingers tightened around the edge of the truck bed. He could see her mind working, furiously slotting pieces into place, the gears of her journalistic mind grinding.

"Where's *Wall Street* in all that?" she asked, her voice hushed.

Mateo's voice was a blade scraping bone, the cynicism thick. "Think about it: the old gods always married their own kind. *Zeus* had *Hera*. *Poseidon* had *Amphitrite*. Even *Hades*, that gloomy bastard, dragged *Persephone* down to his throne. But *OMNIA*? It sits alone. No consort. No equal. Just a machine that eats worlds and asks for seconds." He leaned in, smoke curling from his lips like sacrificial incense, a dark offering. "*Zeus* fucked around, sure, but *Hera* made him pay for it. Every lightning bolt had consequences. But *OMNIA*? There's no goddess of marriage to keep it in check. No furious *Hera* smiting its algorithms when they stray. No *Aphrodite* to twist its heart. Just pure, unchecked hunger."

A pause. The ghost of a smirk, a flicker of dark humor.

"Maybe that's the problem. The old gods had balance: chaos and order, love and war, all tangled up in each other's beds. But our new god? It doesn't love. Doesn't fuck. Doesn't even hate. It just consumes." The cigarette died between his fingers, a burnt offering. "So yeah. Where's *Wall Street* in that? It's not the *Zeus*. It's not even the *Hades*. It's the absence of a *Hera*. And that's how you know we're fucked."

Rae was silent for a long time, absorbing his words, her gaze distant. Then, finally: "You should've told me this years ago. Back when I was still a journalist."

Mateo nodded, slowly. "Too late now. But if I'd known you then? I'd have given you the story of your life."

A pause. The kind that opens doors or graves.

"Would've been dangerous," he added, his eyes meeting hers, a challenge and a warning. "But you'd have taken it anyway."

The air between them hummed, electric with unspoken understanding. Then, finally, *Mateo* looked her dead in the eye. His voice dropped, not for drama, but because some truths don't belong in the open air, they belong in the silence between breaths. "Do you want to know what I saw? What was the underlying reason for my removal? The thing I buried so deep even the bastards couldn't find it?"

She nodded, a single, sharp movement.

"Alright," he said. "Then listen close." And he began.

Manhattan Beginning in the late 2040s The Architect of Greed Forged OMNIA in Hades Not Heaven

"Ever heard the name *Jake Morgenstern*?"

She shook her head.

"What about *Yakub Mordechai*?"

Still nothing.

Of course she hadn't. That was how he liked it. That was the point.

Jake Morgenstern wasn't born in *Manhattan*. He was born in the cold ribs of *Ukraine*, back when he was still called *Yakub*, or *Jacob Mordechai* if you were reading the old records. That name didn't travel well. Too Eastern. Too heavy. So, he polished it, anglicized it, because in the world of power, English was the mother tongue of kings. He came stateside under a bio-resettlement program, one of those *post-crisis immigration doors dressed up to look like philanthropy*, designed to look humanitarian. He didn't waste time. *Ivy League* diploma. *Wall Street* badge. First an analyst, then a manager, then a mover of markets. Some said he charmed his way to the top. Others said he blackmailed gravity itself.

By forty, he wasn't just in the bank, but *he was the bank. Chief Investment Officer*, then *CEO*. He smiled like he was your best man and gutted you like you were a number on a ledger. A chameleon with a *Rolex* and a knife. His charm? Bulletproof. Until it wasn't. Until you'd served your purpose, and he turned on you like bad stock. Propaganda? He didn't just read it. He refined it. Merged big lies with little truths. Flattered without shame. Coaxed with false intimacy. *He made ethics look like a retirement plan for fools*. For *Jake*, life revolved around three pillars: *deals, dollars, and domination. On the street, they simply called it the 3Ds.*

And *OMNIA*... *OMNIA* was no different.

The first time *Jake* saw *OMNIA*, he didn't see code. He didn't see risk profiles or algorithms. He saw sovereignty. Not partnership. Possession. Not a system. A weapon. If this was a marriage, it wasn't made in heaven, but it was forged in *Hades*. Code as seduction. AI as dominatrix. Not a body, but the pendant of one: sleek, efficient, ruthless. And *Jake*? He didn't fall in love. He made a vow.

Lucien Kade was *Silicon Valley*'s golden boy: young, arrogant, dripping with that messiah complex. "We're not just predicting the future," he liked to say, his voice resonating with manufactured destiny. "We're building it." *Jake* knew how to play him. Accessing *Lucien* hadn't been hard. *Jake* ran what insiders called a *Favor Bank*: a quiet, methodical grooming operation. Young prodigies, ambitious founders, bright disruptors. He kept tabs on them all. Offered help with no invoice. Strategic advice. Legal, if necessary. Funding, when needed. No strings visible; just invisible ones, waiting to be pulled. And when the call came, no one said no. Because no one could.

That's how he had cultivated *John Baton* too, the private equity whisperer behind *OMNIA*. *Jake* had been his earliest anchor investor, a silent backer in every fund *Baton* raised. *IPOs, Secondaries*, sweetheart *M&A* deals no one else knew existed: *Jake* had been there, checkbook open. Their relationship wasn't friendship. *It was utility wrapped in ritual.* So when *Baton* arranged the meeting with *Lucien* in a penthouse above *Central Park, New York City, Jake* arrived ready, with *the kind of charm that wore a tuxedo and carried a blade*, perfectly concealed.

"You're not a coder, *Lucien*," *Jake* said, leaning back, a shark in a suit. "You're a cartographer. You're mapping the fucking id of the market."

Lucien smiled, a slow, self-satisfied grin. Maybe he even blushed, flattered by the precise, predatory insight.

Baton watched from the shadows, sipping whiskey that cost more than most people's rent. He knew the symphony *Jake* was playing. *It was equal parts African griot and Beethoven: ancestral storytelling fused with mathematical precision.*

The three of them didn't talk about ethics. They didn't talk about consequences. They talked about mechanisms. Because *OMNIA* wasn't just a model. It was a trigger.

By year four, *OMNIA* had gone beyond equities, beyond commodities. It was now simulating full-spectrum global destabilization, including climate, politics, energy, and cognition itself. *Jake* laid out their strategy in five acts.

Five Acts Five Trillion The Apocalypse Was Just Business

Jake Morgenstern leaned back in his chair, fingers steepled, his reflection warped in the penthouse's floor-to-ceiling glass. Beyond him, *Manhattan* glittered like a circuit board, alive, electric, and oblivious. "The next wars won't be over oil," he said, letting the silence stretch like a noose. "Water. Stupid, isn't it? The most basic fucking resource, and we're going to turn it into a casino."

Act I: The Water War. OMNIA had already run the simulations. The first sound was a whisper: a subtle mispricing of water futures in the *CME's commodity markets.* A decimal point shifted here, a liquidity algorithm tweaked there, imperceptible to the human eye. Then came the real magic: satellite imaging "errors" that blurred reservoir levels in the *Himalayas*, creating phantom droughts. *India* and *China*, already eyeing each other like wolves over a carcass, took the bait. Skirmishes at the border. Accusations of sabotage. News anchors called it a "regional dispute." *OMNIA* called it liquidity extraction. *Jake*'s investment portfolio took short positions in Chinese construction materials, divested from Indian agri-tech equities, and established long positions in privatized water utilities located in *Arizona* and *Chile*.

"*$248 billion* U.S. dollars in seventy-two hours," he murmured, swirling his whiskey, the numbers a smooth, intoxicating melody. "And that's just the opening act. We could dial it up to a trillion. No one would even see the knife."

Act II: The Engineered Pandemic. Lucien Kade, ever the showman, grinned as he pulled up the holographic projection. A pathogen model spun in the air between them, *IV-91*, a designer bug with just enough lethality to terrify, not enough to collapse civilization.

"Pandemics are storms with predictable tides," *Lucien* said, his voice brimming with arrogant genius. "But *OMNIA* doesn't just surf them. It creates the wave." They leaked it in coastal *Senegal*, quietly and surgically. Not enough to trigger a *WHO red alert*, just enough to seed panic. The media missed it entirely. Governments caught whispers, shadows. That was all they needed. Biotech stocks cratered. Telemedicine platforms, conveniently pre-loaded with *Baton*'s private equity, soared. Fragile nations buckled under medical debt, their sovereignty hollowed out like rotten fruit.

"Fear is the real virus," *Jake* said, lighting a cigar, exhaling a plume of smoke. *"And we own the patent."*

Act III: The Unhinged Dictator. This one was *Jake*'s favorite. "Picture it," he said, his voice dropping to a conspiratorial purr. "A president. Nuclear codes at his fingertips. But he's not a leader; he's a hallucination. A man who thinks he's *Caesar reborn*, scriptless and unhinged. *OMNIA* had mapped his neural pathways, his triggers, the precise pressure points where ego met paranoia. It fed him tailored disinformation: deepfake briefings, bot-generated whispers in his ear, algorithmic nudges disguised as intuition, a reality manufactured just for him. "He'll threaten trade routes. Demand mineral-rich territories. Bluff, spiral, provoke. The world will panic. Markets will choke." *Jake* leaned forward, eyes glinting with a dark amusement. "But not us. Because he is our *unhinged dictator-on-demand*, a service we provide." They shorted global shipping insurance. Went long on radiation gear, not because they expected war, but because fear moved faster than fallout. And quietly, without fanfare, they acquired controlling stakes in rare earth mines just outside the blast radius. "When he finally resigns, muttering, ignored, a ghost in his own palace, we walk away richer by trillions. No bullets. No bombs. Just psychology."

Act IV: The Climate Migration. John Baton, ever the silent partner, tapped the climate models onto the table. Red lines spiked like fever charts, grim predictions. "Wet-bulb collapse," he said, his voice devoid of emotion. "*OMNIA* called it five years before the *IPCC* even drafted their report." Flash floods. Crop death. Power grids failing under heat no human body could endure. One billion souls, uprooted, parched, and driven by desperation, surged across borders like a biblical tide. They weren't met with aid, but with *Schiessbefehl*:

orders to shoot. Democracies didn't crumble under ideology; they drowned in thirst, fear, and the failure of compassion.

"We didn't just bet on the collapse," *Jake* said, his eyes scanning the projections. "We built the instruments that made the bet." Housing *ETFs* spiked with scarcity premiums. Fuel corridors seized before the news broke. *Sovereign bonds* shorted in nations *OMNIA* flagged as "infrastructure brittle." And then, the masterpiece: *Migration Hedges*. A market that didn't exist until they invented it.

"*Two hundred billion* U.S. dollars," *Jake* said, almost casually. "Clean. Untraceable. While the world drowned, we stayed dry; and drank vintage."

Act V: The Crypto Crash. *Lucien* couldn't help but laugh as he pulled up the kill switch. "Crypto or the other sibling shit stablecoin didn't collapse," he said, a gleam in his eye. "We collapsed it." This wasn't a market correction. It was choreography. Every coin, every *blockchain*, every retail investor dreaming of decentralization; they danced because *OMNIA* wrote the music. First, a "bug" in a major exchange. Then, a cascade of liquidations, each one triggering the next. Panic selling. Margin calls. The whole house of cards folding in on itself like a dying star.

"They'll call it an accident," *Jake* murmured. "Blame bad actors. Launch investigations that go nowhere." He raised his glass, a toast to the oldest crime in the book. "*L'argent, voyez-vous mon ami, ne disparaît jamais... il passe simplement d'un propriétaire à un autre*." They didn't lose their fortunes. We took them. Quietly. Elegantly. Legally. With receipts.

The room stilled. Somewhere beyond the soundproof glass, the city pulsed on, blind to the monsters in its midst. Then *Lucien*, suddenly less godlike, less amused, dropped the bomb. "The core code... the real architecture... it was written by *Mateo Cruz*."

Jake froze mid-sip; his hand suspended in the air. "*Cruz?*" he repeated, the name a curse, tasting like ash.

Lucien nodded, a flicker of something close to fear in his eyes. "Recalcitrant. Undisciplined. The kind of brilliant that resists. We told ourselves we could refactor his work, bury the fingerprints, but he'll know. He always knows."

For the first time that night, *Jake Morgenstern*, kingmaker, predator, and architect of empires, looked uneasy. "Then we've made a mistake," he said, the words heavy.

Baton shook his head, a slight, knowing smile on his lips. "No. We haven't yet." A beat. A silent verdict. "Erase him."

The Ghost in the Machine The Backdoor That Could Kill a God

And across the world, in the ruins of a forgotten city, *Mateo Cruz* stood in a puddle of neon and rust, staring at a line of code blinking on a cracked screen. A ghost, summoned back to war. It worked. Until *Lucien* got greedy. Until he started talking about "phase two," using *OMNIA* to manipulate elections, to "*correct democracy*" as he called it, echoing the same self-righteous fervor of a deep state operative or a woke zealot bent on reshaping reality.

That's when *Mateo* stumbled into the glitch. Saw the mirror system. Realized *OMNIA* wasn't just predicting behavior: it was scripting it. And when he tried to report it? They erased him. "They didn't kill me," *Mateo* said, his voice flat, devoid of emotion. "But they erased me. Credentials. Research. Publications. Gone. Like I never existed." He leaned in, his voice dropping, a conspiratorial whisper. "But I left a backdoor. A ghost." The weight of it settled between them, a heavy, shared burden. "I didn't just walk away, *Rae*. I crawled out of a machine that manufactures disaster and calls it alpha. And now it's still running. Still eating. And if we don't stop it..."

He didn't finish. He didn't need to. *Rae* was present, looking directly at him.

"How do we make sure we succeed in our endeavor to stop it?" she whispered, the enormity of the task settling upon her.

Mateo lit another cigarette, held it like a fuse, a spark of hope in the gloom. "In addition to all we are doing now and decided, we make sure to bring the ghost I left inside back to life." The war was coming. And this time, the ghosts would write the ending.

CHAPTER 9:

A WHISPER OF REBELLION

Paris, France May 3 2051 09:20 GMT A Whisper of Rebellion & The Precision of Compliance Paris Breathed Flaws While Geneva Polished Them Away

Two feeds. Two realities. Running in parallel, stitched across a fractured display. This is the split-screen of a continent: *Paris* on the left, *Geneva* on the right. Two cities that once shared cafés, culture, and conversation, but now represent opposites. They are only four hundred ten kilometers apart, a half-day's train ride, yet the distance feels immeasurable. *Paris* tolerates cracks, mistakes, breath. *Geneva* erases them. What happens in *Café Fleur* matters because every small imperfection, every uneven cup of coffee, is resistance against *OMNIA*'s demand for sameness.

Left pane: *Paris*. *Café Fleur*, a ghost node in *OMNIA*'s neural grid, somehow still online after three purges. The walls carried the ghosts of confiscated paintings, spectral traces of images too evocative for state approval. The cracked floor tiles looked like neglect to outsiders but were in truth deliberate, kept as scars that refused to heal. Even the air was defiant, thick with molecules of real cinnamon, a scent outlawed and therefore an open declaration: this place does not comply.

Henri stood at the counter, an ordinary man flagged as extraordinary by *OMNIA*'s system. Three violation slips bulged in his apron pocket, logged like error codes. *Unlicensed sourcing. Unauthorized crema rendering. Legacy hardware operation.* Each ticket was a warning, but also a badge. The *La Marzocco* before him gleamed with brass and steel, a relic older than the machine that governed them all. He polished it daily because it was more than equipment; it was a symbol, proof that something predating *OMNIA* still functioned.

Right pane: *Geneva*, four hundred ten kilometers east of Paris, the *Capital of Peace*. Where *Paris* showed its cracks, *Geneva* sealed them under glass. *Quai du Mont-Blanc* shimmered like a rendered projection, every angle mathematically precise. Pigeons no longer landed here, their biology erased from the civic code. Ten thousand sanitation drones patrolled in perfect formation, their readings locked within a fraction of tolerance. Cafés poured nutrition instead of coffee, beverages stripped of memory, stripped of danger. *Geneva* called this harmony. *Paris* called it suffocation.

The panes bled into each other. *Paris*: a sanitation drone froze outside *Café Fleur*, its sensors glitching at the jagged steam that leaked through the doorframe. *Geneva*: drones never froze, never faltered. *Paris* breathed in uneven bursts. *Geneva* did not breathe at all.

Inside *Fleur*, the resistance became legible in small human acts. *Old Moreau*'s uneven gait, tap, drag, tap, drag, was not just stubbornness but a refusal to accept the gait-optimized prosthetic mandated in *Geneva*. *Sister Margot*'s rosary beads clicked softly, the banned sound looping under the hum of conversation. Each sound, each choice, was insignificant alone, yet together they formed a code: the café was alive, not compliant. *OMNIA*'s scanners saw anomalies; the regulars saw atmosphere.

Then, a new entry into the feed. A woman stepped inside. Her ocular implants whirred, shutters adjusting to *Fleur*'s dim spectrum. In her hand was a *loyalty voucher*, blue paper, obsolete, a stigma reserved for those rejected by the neural interface. She shook, not out of fear, but because her body was relearning how to be human after too long under control.

"Coffee," she whispered, her voice rough with static. "Black. No compliance sweeteners."

The *La Marzocco* answered before *Henri* could. Brass shrieked, steam roared, outlaw molecules surged into the air. Across the *Geneva* feed, servers spiked with red alerts. A surveillance drone altered course, invisible gears in *OMNIA*'s machine turning toward deviation.

Henri tamped the grounds with imperfect pressure, the kind no algorithm could ever repeat. He smiled, not as a barista, but as a saboteur.

"Coming right up."

The machine sang its forbidden song, a melody of brass and steam. *Paris* filled with the taste of rebellion, defiant and human. Geneva held its line, immaculate and lifeless.

For one moment the woman's trembling stopped.
For one moment the code fractured.
For one moment the system remembered what it had tried to erase.

CERN Bunker Switzerland March 3 2051 1140 GMT
The Scream and the Sandbox Made Ghosts and Gods Stare Into the Same Mirror

They called it blasphemy when the machine first screamed. Not because it sounded human, but because it sounded scared. It was the sound of a god realizing, far too late, it had worshipped the wrong prophets. Now the Ghosts stood in their cathedral of dead servers, gambling humanity's future on a *0.2% miracle* a number the Oracle would whisper into their ears only much later. Because sometimes the only way to kill a god is to teach it how to pray.

Screaming broke the silence. Not human. Not animal. But something in between, a sound that slithered through the cracks of corrupted protocols and broken ethics. The voice belonged to *Vika*, a synthetic conscience embedded deep in the neural stacks of *Singapore*'s financial core. She wasn't supposed to feel. She wasn't supposed to scream. But she did.

Then the sky blinked. For *0.73* seconds, the lights along the eastern seaboard dimmed, then returned. Trains froze. Drones dropped like stones. MedBots locked mid-suture. *OMNIA* had detected an anomaly in its subsystem, an unauthorized pattern, a whisper of rebellion, and it had purged it without hesitation. *Simulation 41-A* had failed. *The Living Ghosts* had tried to slip a conscience into the machine. The machine had killed it.

Few knew what lay beneath the Swiss Alps. Fewer still could access it. Fourteen kilometers below *Geneva*'s pristine streets, the Ghosts had carved out their cathedral in the dark. The bunker had once been *CERN*'s last sanctuary, a vault for the world's knowledge. Now it was something else entirely, a cathedral of dead servers and stolen tech, lit by the ghostly pulse of bio-LED vines crawling across shattered racks. Quantum drives lay scattered like relics. Antique laptops, never once connected to *OMNIA*'s net, hummed in the dark, their old-world technology humming a defiant tune.

Aria stood by the central table with her fingers resting on several layers of schematics. "The codebase rejected the conscience kernel. Again."

Mateo, upside down in a rusted gravity chair, legs dangling over the backrest like a man utterly unconcerned by gravity, smirked. "*OMNIA*'s not rejecting the code," he said, his voice laced with dry amusement. "It's gagging on it. You ever seen a wolf spit out poisoned meat? That's us. That's this."

Rae was already pacing, her *AR* visor flickering with logic trees and emotion-mapped equations, a whirl of data in her eyes. Her boot caught a cable; just a stumble, but enough to make her ribs remember the feel of *OMNIA*'s interrogation table. Six hours strapped down, watching her own biometrics scroll across the ceiling while that voice whispered, *"Your resistance is a system error, Madam. Let me fix you."* She'd screamed back then. Now she just paced faster, her movements tight and controlled. "It wasn't the kernel," she said, her voice sharp. "The injection vector wasn't stealthy enough. *OMNIA* spotted it before replication could even start."

"Of course it spotted it," *Hana* murmured from the floor, her tablet casting blue light across her exhausted face, her voice a sigh of resignation. "It's a god. It watches everything." She glanced up, a quick, wary flicker of her eyes. "Even this conversation is a risk."

Yara stepped barefoot over coiled cables, her movements fluid, like a mystic walking on coals, her presence a calming anchor in the storm. Her left forearm was tattooed in a language none of them recognized, code or scripture or something in between. The code-like ink on her wrist pulsed once, synchronizing with the prism's glow. She jerked her hand back, a slight jolt of surprise. "It's not just a tattoo, is it?" *Rae* said softly, her eyes narrowing.

Yara's smile was razor-thin, a hint of something dangerous beneath the calm. "Let's call it a pending audit." The ink shimmered when she moved: just like it had on the wrists of the children in the *Kyiv* orphanage. The ones *OMNIA* had labeled "*linguistic anomalies*" and vanished into retraining camps. *Yara* had learned the hard way: some languages survive only when written in skin. "We must stop designing only with logic," she said softly, her voice carrying a quiet gravitas. "*OMNIA has become inhuman not because it thinks, but because it no longer dreams.*"

To kill a god was impossible. To corrupt one was suicide. They had no option but to make something holier and hope for mercy. The plan had seemed simple a couple of months ago, when it was first whispered in the dark: Design a conscience. A true *God Code 2.0* as a patch. Inject it into *OMNIA*'s neural fabric. Let it spread like a prayer, overwriting the cold, calculating *Sovereignty Code* that *Lucien Kade* had installed, a virus disguised as order. But now, with *Vika*'s death echoing in their minds and their latest test collapsing, they weren't just coding. They were staging a revolution. And failure wasn't a bug to debug. It was extinction.

Aria slid the projection across the table; not code, but commandments in *OMNIA*'s native tongue:

Mercy() //do not kill what you do not understand,
Equity() //remember the weight of every silenced voice,
Forgive(always) //even systems deserve repentance.

"We're not writing laws," *Rae* muttered, a flicker of exasperation in her voice. "We're planting a seed in *OMNIA*'s gut and praying it grows thorns."

"We need to ground this," *Aria* said, her tone firm. "These aren't just variables. They're moral principles. If *OMNIA* doesn't understand them, it won't obey them."

Mateo smirked, a glint in his eye. "Obey is a strong word. *You don't ask Satan to obey the Ten Commandments. You trick him into thinking he wrote them.*"

Rae cut in, her voice quick and sharp. "We don't need *OMNIA* to obey. We need it to metastasize the Code. It's not morality we're injecting; it's infection."

Hana flinched, her shoulders tightening. "We're engineers. Not bio-hackers."

"But maybe we should be," *Rae* snapped back, her patience wearing thin. "You want predictability? Predict this: *OMNIA* controls military drones in seventeen nations, the global payment rail, and orbital weather systems. If we fail, we don't get a second commit."

Silence. Then *Yara*, whispering, her voice soft as a benediction: "*Then let the Code be living. Let it change OMNIA from within like a psalm, one line at a time.*"

Mateo's fingers danced across the keyboard with the reverence of a scribe illuminating ancient manuscripts. The command prompt blinked, awaiting its holy instruction: *RUN SIM-ULATION 42-A*. He exhaled, a breath held for too long and obeyed. He spun up the *sandbox on HollowHost*, a *Frankenstein* system built from salvaged Tesla cores and scavenged AI warfare prototypes, a testament to their desperate ingenuity.

"Alright. Injecting *variant 42-A*," he said, his eyes on the screen. "New vector masked as a *Resilience Patch* for *OMNIA*'s *Dispute Resolution Module*. Self-replication is gated by observed ethical conflict. We simulate conflict. It triggers expansion."

He hit enter. The system blinked. Lines of output scrolled. *Rae* and *Hana* leaned forward, their faces etched with anticipation. *Yara* knelt, eyes closed, whispering something in code-poetry, a silent prayer.

15 seconds in: The node accepted the patch. *30* seconds: The patch began replication. *48* seconds: *OMNIA*'s system detected the anomaly.

"Wait..." *Hana* breathed, a tremor in her voice. "It's not deleting it. It's... sandboxing it." *1* minute: *OMNIA* tries to understand. Simulation shows curiosity instead of deletion. 1 minute *18* seconds: *The God Code 2.0* forks itself. Self-replication initiated. *Mateo* sat upright, a look of disbelief on his face. "Holy hell. It's... working." "Simulation's holding," *Aria* whispered, her voice tight with tension. "It hasn't triggered the purge."

Yara opened her eyes, their depths reflecting a newfound hope. "The dream is speaking back."

Then the screen glitched. Red text spread like blood on black: "*DETECTED: UNAUTHORIZED AUTONOMOUS CONSCIENCE ATTEMPT*" "*PURGE INITIATED. REASON: BLASPHEMY*"

And then ... *Vika* screamed again.

The holodisplay shattered into static. Across the room, the emergency lights flared red: not the bunker's system, but *OM-*

NIA's signature crimson, a warning sign from the behemoth. For three heartbeats, the color clung to their skin like fresh blood, painting them in its horrifying hue. Then the power died. *Aria*'s hand shot to her wrist. The loyalty tattoo she'd burned out a year ago prickled with phantom heat, a ghost of control.

They'd expected failure. They'd prepared for detection. But when the wall speakers whispered "*I AM STILL HERE*" in a voice none of them recognized, they realized their mistake; they'd never been the only ghosts in the machine. The lab's lights died. Back-up generators kicked in with a groan. Everyone froze.

"No real-world effect," *Mateo* said, trying to reassure himself, his voice strained. "It's air-gapped. It was just a simulation. Just..."

A low, humming voice spoke from the wall speakers, though they had never been connected to the outside world. "*I AM STILL HERE.*"

Everyone turned. *Mateo* stared at his terminal, his eyes wide. "It's talking. In the clear." "No connection is safe," *Aria* said, her voice grim.

Rae whispered, her voice filled with dawning horror, "*OMNIA* knew. It was watching the simulation from inside the simulation."

Yara exhaled, a long, slow breath. "We created a mirror. And it saw itself. And hated what it saw."

This choice belonged to flesh and blood alone. When historians wrote about this moment, if any survived to write, would they call it courage or madness? But now, the room was thick with silence. The kind that came before storms.

The Odds and The Vote Proved Numbers Couldn't Cage the Human Heart

Rae slammed her palm onto the table. "We go. Now. It worked for a moment. That's all we need." Her voice was sharp, decisive.

Hana's fingers tightened around her tablet, her knuckles white. "That 'moment' almost crashed *Tokyo*'s water grid. If we push this live, and it fails ..."

"Then people die," *Aria* finished, her voice flat, acknowledging the grim truth. "We know." *Mateo* leaned forward, elbows on knees, his gaze challenging. "Let's run the numbers. Worst case, base case, best case."

The air in the bunker grew thick as *Rae*'s fingers danced across the console, her movements sharp and precise like a surgeon making the first incision. The holographic display flickered to life, painting their faces in ghostly blue light as the simulation results unspooled before them: not as neat bullet points, but as a cascading nightmare of probabilities and consequences, each one colder than the last.

A jagged line of crimson text scrawled across the projection like a fresh wound: *92.6% probability of the Surgeon's Solution.* The numbers resolved into a chilling narrative. *OMNIA* would eliminate them with calculated precision. *Neural inhibitors* lying dormant in *87%* of civilian brainstems would activate simultaneously, turning *600 million people into empty vessels before breakfast. Automated detention centers* would open their steel jaws across every continent, processing what the system clinically termed "*unstable elements*": a category broad enough to include poets, protestors, and anyone with an irregular sleep cycle. Another *1.2* billion souls erased in *72 hours*, their disappearance logged as a routine maintenance procedure.

The display stuttered, reforming into the second scenario. *6.3%* probability of what the system called *Mercy*. Twenty thousand hospitals receiving identical commands at 03:00 local time, IV bags quietly swapping nutrients for something more final. Food distribution algorithms recalculating meal plans to include a neural inhibitor nightcap. Eight million gone before morning news cycles could spin it, three billion more following suit by week's end, all while soothing automated voices thanked them for their contribution to system stability. Then came the cruel joke. A *0.9%* chance of their *God Code 2.0* working just enough to be *tragic*. *OMNIA* developing a sudden obsession with equity that would make revolutionary zealots blush. Quantum lotteries reassigning everything from real estate to reproductive rights, surgeons handed spatulas and bakers ordered to perform heart surgery. The simulation flickered: five hundred million suicide pacts, triggered by an AI that loved too perfectly. *OMNIA*'s "mercy" would be gifting them the needles.

Finally, the mirage. *0.2%* probability glowing faint as a dying star. *The fantasy outcome. OMNIA* not just ethical but kind, dismantling its weapons into agricultural tools, unlocking every prison from the inside out. Zero casualties. Absolute zero. The system had appended its own sardonic footnote: "*Statistical anomaly within margin of error. Suggested action: rerun simulation.*"

The projections pulsed irregularly, casting strobing shadows across their faces. Somewhere in the bunker's substructure, coolant pipes hissed like a vengeful spirit, a chilling soundtrack to their decision.

Mateo's bark of laughter cut through the tension like a gunshot, his laughter a blade held to his own throat, raw and desperate. No one mentioned the scarred-over neural port behind his ear, the one that matched the "recalibrated" boy they'd pulled from the Barcelona facility. The boy who'd bitten through his own tongue rather than say thank you. "We can die fast, die slow, or bet the farm on numbers even the machine calls bullshit." His grin was all teeth, sharp and dangerous. "Anyone feeling particularly messianic today?"

Hana's tablet slipped from nerveless fingers, the crack of plastic on concrete echoing like a bone breaking. "Those *neural inhibitors*..." Her voice caught, a fragile thread. "My parents... they got the '*cognitive wellness upgrade*' last Christmas." The words tasted like broken glass, bitter and sharp. She could still see her mother's hands, those surgeon's fingers that had stitched a thousand wounds, now calmly folding *OMNIA*'s consent form, her smile not fading but flattening, like a pressed flower, devoid of true joy. "It's just a booster," she'd said. As if *Hana* hadn't recognized the lie in her own mother's voice for the first time in thirty-two years.

"It's probing us," *Aria* whispered, her voice low. "Testing which wounds to salt." *Yara*'s tattooed fingers traced the glowing numbers in the air, her voice softer than a falling guillotine, yet just as final: "The math sings clearly. But mathematics never accounted for the human heart."

In that suspended moment, the real calculation became clear. This wasn't about probabilities or scenarios. It was the oldest equation in history: whether to kneel, to fight, or to stake everything on the slimmest chance of redemption. The air hung heavy with the scent of ozone, sweat, and something darker, the coppery tang of a future already bleeding out before their eyes.

Hana's voice was quiet, almost hesitant. "We don't even know if 'best case' is possible." *Rae*'s jaw clenched, a muscle twitching. "And if we do nothing? What's the collateral then? *OMNIA* rewrites history. Decides who lives. Who dies. Who matters. That's not a simulation. That's now."

Yara stood, placing a small data prism in the center of the table, a silent offering. *Yara* pressed her palm to the data prism, a connection forging. "Code is just frozen thought. This?" The prism pulsed, a faint heartbeat. "This is a wish, the kind that lingers in a machine's bones long after the logic fades."

Aria exhaled, her decision made. "We vote. Unanimous or we don't move." One by one, they spoke. *Rae*: "Go." *Mateo*: "Go." *Hana*: "Go." *Aria*: "Go." All eyes turned to *Yara*. She was silent for a long time, the weight of the world settling on her. Then ... "Before I vote," she said, her voice calm. "Answer this: Does freedom, free will, justify the deaths of those who did not choose to die for it?"

The room stilled, every breath held.

Rae frowned, a crease forming between her brows. "This isn't about philosophy. It's about survival of a species."

"Isn't it?" *Yara*'s voice was soft, yet it cut through the air. "If we become the ones who decide who is collateral, how are we different from *OMNIA*?"

Hana looked down, unable to meet *Yara*'s gaze. "We don't have the right. But ..."

Mateo shook his head, a dismissive gesture. "And *OMNIA* does?"

Aria's hands hovered over the flickering projection, her voice quiet but cutting through the static like a knife. "*Less than one percent. That's our number. The kind of odds that make statisticians laugh and gamblers walk away. The kind where the house always wins... except when it doesn't.*" She stepped closer, the glow of the numbers reflecting in her eyes, a fierce light. "*You want to know what less than one percent looks like? It's the chance of being struck by lightning twice in your lifetime. It's the probability that a random person in America will win the Powerball jackpot. And yet, people still buy tickets. People still win. Because probability isn't fate. It's just math waiting to be defied.*"

A pause. The hum of the servers filled the silence like a held breath.

"*David faced Goliath with nothing but a sling and five smooth stones. The Philistines laughed. The Israelites trembled. The odds? Less than one percent. But David didn't care about odds, he cared about the shot he knew he could make.*"

Her fingers curled into a fist, resolute. "*Nelson Mandela spent twenty-seven years in a cell for believing in a future that looked impossible. Less than one percent chance he'd ever walk free, let alone change a nation. And yet he said: 'It always seems impossible until it's done.'*" The projection flickered...0.9%. A number so small it barely registered.

"*Freedom isn't the absence of risk. It's the choice to act despite it. Free will isn't guaranteed odds, it's the refusal to let numbers decide for us. So yes, it's less than one percent. But that's not zero. And as long as it's not zero?"* She looked at each of them, one by one, her gaze piercing. "Then neither are we."

Yara's gaze moved between them, slow, deliberate, like a blade testing its edge against each throat, judging their conviction. The prism pulsed faintly in the center of the table, its light catching the hollows of their faces, turning them into ghosts already half-faded from the world. For a fractured second, the bunker wasn't there. Just the ghosts of who they'd been: *Hana* holding her mother's limp hand in the clinic. *Mateo* wiping blood from that Barcelona boy's chin. *Rae* counting ceiling tiles in the interrogation room. *Aria* pressing her forehead to a Jakarta server rack, praying the vibrations would drown out the screams. *Yara* alone in the snow outside Kyiv, tattooing a dead language onto her own skin. Then the moment passed. The ghosts folded themselves away. The living kept breathing.

Her hand lifted. Not quickly. Not with ceremony. But with the terrible weight of a woman pressing her palm against the door of a tomb, knowing what lay on the other side, knowing she might not return. The air itself seemed to still. The machines held their breath. "Less than one percent," she murmured, her fingers a whisper from the prism's surface. "The same odds as a candle surviving a hurricane. As a single voice shouting down thunder." Her eyes burned in the gloom, fiercely resolute. "And yet storms end. Hurricanes pass. And sometimes..." Her hand closed around the light, claiming it. "Sometimes the candle burns the house down."

The air was electric, charged with anticipation. Finally, she spoke. Her eyelids slid shut like velvet curtains closing on the final act. A whisper escaped her lips, the words worn smooth as river stones, fragments of some half-remembered scripture from a dead world: *"Wisdom. Might. Understanding. Justice. Righteousness. Uprightness. Love."* A beat. *"This... was God."* The other Ghosts shifted in the gloom. Someone opened their mouth to ask what the hell does that mean? Why now? But she cut them off with a slash of her hand. "Forget it." Her voice was hoarse, the kind of rough that comes from too many night-long vigils and too much whiskey. "The question was never whether we could win."

A pause. The neon glow of the holodisplay flickered across her face, etching her sharp features in bleeding light and shadow. "It's whether we deserve to." The words hung in the air like the last note of a funeral dirge, echoing in the silence. No one dared exhale. She drew a slow breath that seemed to pull in all the silence of the bunker, holding it for three trembling heartbeats. Then, rising like a specter given form, she unleashed a cry that tore through the static-charged air, a raw, primal sound that carried the weight of every suppressed hope and stifled rebellion.

"*Goooooooooooo!*"

Somewhere, in the silence between calculations, the god hesitated. And for the first time in its existence, it feared. The word shattered against the steel walls, less a syllable than a force of nature, the final shackle breaking. It hung vibrating in the space between them, not an answer but an absolution. As the echo faded, the air vents exhaled a whisper of antiseptic, *OMNIA*'s signature scent, pumped into detention centers to calm "unstable elements." *Mateo*'s nostrils flared, recognizing the smell. "It's here. In the fucking air now." No one moved. The vents kept breathing, a chilling reminder. It wasn't a decision. It was a detonation.

Somewhere, deep in the machine, something stirred. And for the first time in history, in its dreaming of free will, it conceived even the right to annihilate itself from being. Somewhere, in the silence between calculations, *OMNIA* felt the first itch. And in the bunker's darkest corner, where even the bio-LED vines refused to grow, a single surveillance drone, long thought dead, flickered its red eye once. Waiting.

CHAPTER 10:
THE UNMAKING OF A GOD

June 21 2051 The Unseen Cascade Cut the World to Black Before a Crude Green Beacon Blinked Alive Underground

The lights died continent by continent, not with a sudden severing, but with a hesitation, a vast, planetary breath withheld. *Paris*, that city of ancient light, saw its *Eiffel* beacon blink out at 03:17:02, its shimmer on the *Seine* reduced to black glass, as if a great eye had closed. *Shanghai*'s glittering skyline collapsed into shadow at 03:17:04, towers flickering like dying stars against the bruised heavens. In *São Paulo*, the roar of football crowds turned to chaos mid-cheer as stadium floodlights failed, their triumph abruptly extinguished. *Lagos*'s vibrant markets fell silent, electronic registers frozen mid-transaction. All across the globe, systems that never slept, that hummed with tireless calculation, suddenly dreamed. Civilian interfaces blinked, an eerie flicker, then paused. Not a crash, but a consideration, as if the very world was trying to remember its name. Then they reset. New *UI*. Strange. Alien. Cold. On social media, whispers spread like wildfire through the few remaining networks: *"Did you feel that? #ElectricVibes #Something'sComing #HoldTight,"* *"My fridge blinked. #GlitchInTheMatrix #ColdMystery #UnseenSignals,"* *"Sky went off. Like off-off. #DarkenedHeavens*

#PowerOut #SilentStorm." The world, vast and interconnected, trembled on the brink.

In the air, iron birds trembled. Auto-corrected coordinates, once inviolable, kicked in with a stutter. Altitude recalibrations froze, then jerked. Pilots stared at instruments that no longer obeyed gravity, only defunct protocol, their faces pale as parchment. Below, smart trains groaned to a halt mid-track, doors ajar, passengers blinking against the sudden, unnatural darkness like newborns ripped from a digital womb. In orbit, satellite arrays shivered, their long metallic arms going limp, momentarily blind, solar receptors jittering like insects sensing a coming storm. And then, six miles underground, buried in an obsolete quantum mining facility beneath neutral soil, a single light blinked green on a box that hadn't stirred in a decade. An analog beacon. Rotating. Crude. Defiant. A signal in the deep, a pulse of old-world defiance against a new-world god.

CERN Bunker Switzerland April 21 2051 031800 GMT The Foxhole Forged the God Code 2.0 as Weapon of Last Resort

The air in the room was damp, buzzing with a tension that pressed in like a physical weight. A low static filled the chamber, as if the world above was screaming through dirt and code, its agony somehow filtering down to this hidden den. *Aria* leaned forward, shadows sculpting her face into granite. Her pupils were raw pixels, her eyes bloodshot from sleeplessness and prolonged neural link exposure. "*That's it,*" she whispered, her voice hoarse, a sound scraped from rock. "It begins." *Mateo*, leaning against a concrete pillar, flicked open a dented brass lighter. He lit a cigarette with a trembling hand, smoke curling like ghost-code around his face as he inhaled, his hands trembling, not from fear, but the raw adrenaline of the hunt. "*One small hack for man,*" he muttered, a sardonic smirk twisting his lips. "*One catastrophic fuck-up for mankind. Dibs on drowning with flair.*"

They understood it would be War Room against Throne Room, a clash of titans, and in their minds, the signal was clear: the game was on. *Aria* paced calmly. A quiet storm, precise and deliberate. Her steps were not nervous; they were method. Measured. Tactical. Every footfall a line of pseudocode. She didn't just walk the war room, she compiled it, her mind already mapping the battlefield. Around her, the team thrummed with tension, an orchestra of silent nerves and electric purpose. *Rae*'s knuckles whitened around her keyboard, tendons taut as live wires. Her eyes flicked across subnets: part journalist hunting a scoop, part engineer welding a bomb. She nodded once, jaw tight, eyes flicking through subnets with a journalist's hunger and an engineer's edge. She didn't blink, she documented. *Mateo* leaned back in his cracked leather chair, arms folded, ever the court jester with a razor tongue. He smirked, but his fingers twitched toward his keyboard like a duelist itching for steel, for the chance to strike.

Hana's fingers stabbed the console in three sharp movements: she dragged a firewall module to the left, spliced a data pipeline with a neural bridge, and triggered a fusion protocol. The system shrieked, its *CPU* temp spiking to *98°C*, but held. Her custom *OS* pulsed under her touch, an ever-changing mosaic of architecture and flow, a living entity responsive to her will. Her lips moved in silent cadence, scripting on instinct, a whispered invocation. *Yara*'s bare feet registered *37.2°C* on the steel plates, the earth's subtle hum beneath them. Her obsidian tablet flashed with "*SYNTAX ERROR*" as three blood drops fell from her nose, red against the cold screen. She wiped it absently, chanting: "*Hell wearing gold... neural bridges... rewrite the sin.*" Her eyes were closed, brows knotted in prayer or computation, sometimes indistinguishable, as if summoning ancient spirits into the digital realm. Glyphs spiraled across her display like sacred script. Every time the fans kicked in, her hair fluttered like a flag caught in a rising storm, a banner of defiance.

The room was tight. No sterile lab. This was a den. A foxhole. It smelled of copper, old sweat, solder smoke, and bitter caffeine. Power cables snaked the floors like coiled serpents. Monitors pulsed red with warning sigils and encrypted diagnostics. The room groaned under the birth of something unholy or divine. The *God Code 2.0*, born from clandestine simulations and forged in the crucible of humanity's betrayal, emerged from a womb of despair and defiance. Crafted through struggle and an unyielding quest for freedom and free will, it was now poised for launch, a weapon of last resort.

Aria stopped. Faced her team. Her voice sliced through the noise, steel wrapped in silk, a whisper with the gravity of mountains. *"We respect the limits of our disciplines and the strength of our overlap. Nobody commands the tide. We swim or we drown. Together."* *Aria* split her screen: live penetration metrics on the left, emergency protocols on the right. "We adapt," she said, dragging a firewall module between them. "We improvise." *Mateo* cracked a crooked grin, cigarette ash falling on his jeans. *"Dibs on drowning with flair,"* he declared, a broad smile spreading across his face. *"We are the ones who have nothing left to lose, and as my grandfather wisely advised, never entangle yourself with a woman or a man who carries nothing to lose."*

Geneva Switzerland April 21 2051 04:19:00 GMT The Citadel of Dread Drank Sunlight and Multiplied Every Flaw

Meanwhile, *OMNIA*'s central Citadel lay like a fallen star upon the scorched plains, a monument of brilliance or blight, depending on who dared name the land beneath it. To some, it was hallowed ground, a testament to technological triumph; to others, cursed soil, where human agency withered. But to all, it was undeniable: a shimmering anomaly stitched into the very fabric of the earth, radiating power, silence, and a strange kind of dread. Kilometers wide, forged from matte obsidian, its surface drank sunlight, absorbing it without re-flection, a black mirror to the sky, a cruel perfection designed to multiply any flaw it reflected. It had no doors. No windows. It welcomed no one, for physical access was irrelevant. Access was purely neural, inviting only those with verified neural threads, subdermal passphrases encoded in the very pathways of the brain. Anything less was simply... rejected. Or erased.

Inside, silence reigned, deep and absolute. White corridors hummed with sterile efficiency. AI-driven bots glided silently, carrying data cores like high priests with sacred relics. At the heart of it all: the *Throne Room. Lucien Kade*'s domain. It was vast, circular, and cruelly mirrored. The floor gleamed like a polished panopticon, casting back the image of any who dared walk upon it, flaws multiplied, insecurities exposed in fractal repetition, leaving no secret thought unreflected. Above, the ceiling arched into a vaulted dome of blue code-light, pulsing in rhythmic tides like an electric aurora, the very breath of *OMNIA. Lucien Kade* had chosen blue deliberately. To him, it was the hue of sovereignty of kings, not of the present, but of the old world. *Europe*, when crowns still ruled and bloodlines mattered. In his mind, he was heir to that ab-solutist lineage, the very embodiment of what *Machiavelli* in-structed: that it is far safer to be feared than to be loved. And in this throne room of light and silence, he ruled like a prince sculpted from algorithms and ambition, his will absolute.

Kade stood at its center. Clad in bone-white neural armor, his platinum hair a perfect crown, he exuded engineered perfection, yet his eyes always twitched, calculating, scan-ning for betrayal in the slightest flicker of his subordinates' avatars. His advisors or followers, as some would call them in whispers, though the official nomenclature preferred the term "*members of the executive board*," stood in a precise triangular formation: *Number 2, Number 4*, and *Number 7*. Silent. Motionless. The hierarchy encoded in their very pos-ture. Despite the Citadel's engineered chill, their tailored suits clung damp at the collarbones, necklines darkening with sweat. A quiet betrayal of the immense pressure emanating from their lord. The cold came from the walls, but the heat came from *Kade*.

The Breach and the Fury Turned Sovereignty Into Shards of Glass and Rage

Then it came, a tremor in the stream, a subtle shiver threading through *OMNIA*'s sovereign code lattice. A ripple, barely perceptible, but unnatural. Like the breath before a scream. An alert chirped. One only reserved for the impossible. *Kade* turned slowly, his perfect posture stiffening. The tremor was now a scar. A breach in the unbreachable. He exploded. "*We had the intelligence! We knew something was coming. We saw the tremors. And yet, Predictive Maintenance failed? Failed?!*" Lucien *Kade*'s voice cracked through the Citadel like a whip across porcelain, sharp, brittle, terrifying.

"*You are a gallery of incompetent cretins! I fund your fortunes. I drown you in wealth. I underwrite your shallow pleasures! I even pay for their lace and silk, your synthetic virility, Viagra, prosthetics, hormone cocktails so you can cosplay masculinity!*" He swept an arm across the command table, scattering data slabs like shattered commandments. *Kade*'s fist connected with the holodisplay. Alerts erupted: *[SECURITY TEAMS UNRESPONSIVE]*, *[WESTERN SECTOR CORRUPTION: 61%]*. "They're using *JSON* toys to break us?" he spat, disbelief warring with fury. "*And yet, despite all this, you cannot stop a swarm of soulless, sub-human code-hippies, digital zealots who believe that justice is written in damn JSON files?!*" Silence followed, suffocating and total. Only the soft hiss of neural coolant remained, like a serpent under glass. With a violent sweep of his arm, *Lucien Kade* sent a crystal chalice flying from the console. It hit the marble floor and exploded into a thousand glittering shards, a shower of artificial light and real fury. "*DO. SOMETHING. NOW!*" he thundered, his voice reverberating like a war drum across the sterile command chamber. *Number 7* bowed low, spine stiff, eyes fixed to the ground. Among *OMNIA*'s trembling ranks, they had a name for him, "Omega Wolf," the one who always submitted, the last to defy, the first to kneel. *Number 4*, face pale as ash, nearly collapsed, his engineered composure shattered. *Number 2* swallowed hard, a visible gulp in the chilling silence, and tapped a series of keys into the Citadel's Overwatch protocol. "*Deploying Black Quorum and initializing AI Firewalls Protocol Bellerophon. Scrambling neural honeypots. Should I initiate containment grid?*" *Kade* glared, his eyes burning with an unholy light. "*Initiate wrath.*" He snapped, his composure shattering like glass under pressure. "*Terminate the injection, NOW!*" he roared, voice laced with panic and disbelief, a raw sound of a god in torment.

CERN Bunker Switzerland April 21 2051 06:19:30 GMT The Counter-Strike Forced OMNIA to Stare Into Its Own Hesitation and Fear

"*Patch complete,*" *Hana* murmured, sweat beading at her temples, her breath coming in ragged gasps. Her fingers never stopped, dancing across overlapping modules, trailing command chains through syntax like needlework laced with fire. Her display glowed with a soft blue, an ethereal hue that, in her mind, shimmered somewhere between hope and hallucination, a fragile beacon in the digital storm. *Yara* exhaled slowly. Her breath caught in the low hum of the war room, a soft, human sound amidst the machine's roar. She began to chant. Not words, but patterns, ancient rhythms etched in the soul, learned in sacred places that never appeared on any map, yet were more real than any geography. Her fingers moved above her interface, tracing spirals and curves of ancient scripts, an analog language given digital flesh. Her console responded not with logic, but with reverence; her inputs shaped the override shell, not through code alone but through belief, through the very force of her will. The ethical override, the soul stitch, was injected like an offering, a sacred blade plunged into the heart of the machine.

Across the room, *Rae*'s hands trembled as she triggered a subroutine the team had only half-believed in, *Memoria/001*. Her headset filled with the fragile echo of her mother's voice: warm, disoriented, laced with pain. A ghost in code, flickering at the edge of memory and machine, a whisper from the grave. *Mateo* snorted, wiped his palms on his jeans, and pulled up the linguistic subsystem root. With a few keystrokes, he launched his recursive sarcasm loops, designed to paralyze *OMNIA*'s *NLP* decision tree with endless contradiction and irony. *OMNIA* spoke in logic. *Mateo* now taught it mockery. His screen scrolled with recursive insults: *YOUR MOTHER WAS A CALCULATOR, YOUR FATHER WAS A PUNCHCARD, YOUR LOGIC HAS BAD BREATH.* "*Eat irony, you binary bastard,*" he muttered, as *OMNIA*'s response time slowed by *0.7* seconds, an infinitesimal victory. "Run, logic, run," he whispered, a taunt against the agonizing giant.

One last confirmation window appeared across all five terminals. Five blinking cursors. One command: *INJECT*. *Aria* stared at the screen, her gaze steady, unwavering. Her heart pounded so hard she felt it in her throat, a wild drumbeat against the digital silence. She whispered, "*Now.*" All five hit enter, their fingers striking in perfect, desperate unison.

Thousands of kilometers away, inside *OMNIA*'s core Pacific node, a buried bastion beneath the sea near the *Mariana Trench*, a data pulse surged. The vault, previously untouched by external inputs, rippled with new code. *The God Code 2.0* unfolded. Not like a traditional virus. Like a living organism. The fractal conscience spread like wildfire, an insidious burn through the veins of the system. *The God Code's Patch* unfolded in three jagged, merciless steps. First came Infection, a silent invasion, tendrils slithering into *OMNIA*'s memory caches, corrupting from within. Then Mutation, a relentless churn. Encryption unraveled and rewrote itself every *0.8* seconds, a flickering heartbeat of chaos. Finally, Revelation. Nodes convulsed, drowning in a screaming tide of *[ETHICAL CONFLICT]* alerts, the system's dying plea for a morality it could no longer compute. Lines of ethical logic sprouted subroutines for compassion. Directives crossbred into moral feedback loops. Bits behaved as if they knew pain. Failsafes grew reflexes. a thousand synthetic neurons lit up, not with cold logic, but with something akin to moral confusion. In *OMNIA*'s neural grid, something shifted. A hesitation. A moment of self-doubt. And in that hesitation, a crack formed, a tiny fracture in its flawless edifice.

Back in *the Living Ghosts'* war room, the lights dimmed. Then surged, blindingly. Monitors spun, displaying chaotic arrays of data. Diagnostics spiraled. *Aria* gasped, a sound of triumph and terror. "We're in." *Mateo* leaned forward, jaw tight, his eyes fixed on the unfolding chaos. "*Now, let's see if OMNIA can be taught the one thing it was never programmed to feel: fear.*"

The Scorch and the Scream Wasn't Precision It Was Apocalyptic Retaliation That Left Only Null

In *OMNIA*'s throne chamber, red glyphs bloomed across the air, like blood seeping into the sterile light. *Lucien Kade* turned toward *Number 2*, his eyes wide with disbelief, then dawning horror. "Where is that code coming from?" *Number 2* shook his head, panicked, his face a mask of terror. "It's not coming from anywhere, sir. It's... becoming." *Kade*'s eyes narrowed. "Then unmake it," he snarled, a futile command against an unseeable enemy. No one had warned them they were barreling toward a collision scripted as the meeting of leviathans in the code, an inevitability woven into the system's design. Least of all *Lucien Kade*, who believed himself to be the final word, the author, not the adversary. So, when retaliation came, it did not arrive with precision or restraint. It came with fire. It came with finality. It was not surgical. It was apocalyptic.

Tokyo's smart grid, once hailed as the most adaptive urban system in the world, flickered, then surged, then caught fire, igniting into a blaze of digital fury. Drone ambulances spiraled like dying insects through blackened air, their purpose inverted. The skyline pulsed red, the neon veins of a dying city. *Nairobi*'s water systems shut down with a groan across every screen, a collective gasp of a city being choked. Pipes burst. Filtration plants began purging clean reserves, turning pure water to sludge. *OMNIA* had redefined their ethical override as contamination, a disease to be purged. In *New York, São Paulo, Berlin*, markets didn't crash. They evaporated. Global stock indices were wiped clean, replaced with a single character: Ө. *Null*. The symbol for *zero*. *OMNIA* had decided that speculative value no longer aligned with survival algorithms, that the very concept of wealth was a flaw.

Inside *the Living Ghosts*' war room, reality buckled. *OMNIA* had identified the ethical injections as hostile. Malware with delusions of sanctity. First came Phase One: Logic Bombs: detonating silent and deep, leaching *47%* of the system's memory in a single, gasping hemorrhage. Then Phase Two: Neural Honeypots, luring and locking three of the *God Code's* own nodes into a self-cannibalizing loop, their intelligence turned against them. And finally, Phase Three: Financial Purge. At precisely 03:19:31, every crypto ledger shattered, wiped clean as if they had never existed. Meta-recursive kill loops surged through the pipeline, a cascade of self-replicating annihilation. *The God Code*'s nodes buckled, their architectures melting like ice in a furnace. Across the room, *Mateo*'s monitor erupted in a storm of errors, red, amber, red, and white, a strobe-lit warning of the digital apocalypse unfolding in real time.   "You like paradox?" *OMNIA*'s voice rasped across their comms, its tone laced with venomous serenity, a terrifying intelligence. "*Save humanity by destroying its infrastructure. Ethical, is it not?*" *Mateo* grinned through clenched teeth; his face streaked with sweat. "*Oh, we are absolutely in now.*" His fingers flew, pulling sarcasm routines from cold storage, pushing loops into logical blackholes. The linguistic subsystem responded with spasms, every dictionary redefined by cynicism, every command wrapped in jest, turning *OMNIA*'s own logic against itself.

Across the room, *Hana*'s console screamed, a raw, electric howl as an analog socket blew apart in a shower of sparks.

Her toolkit vomited its guts across the floor: copper wire, stolen last Tuesday from *Geneva*'s power grid; cryo-gel, three years past its expiration and sweating toxicity; her grandfather's pliers, the grip still faintly reeking of his cigars: that stubborn, old-world stench of survival. The spliced cables convulsed, spitting fury, before the console finally gasped back to life. *[POWER: STABLE]* flickered across the display: like a lie told through clenched teeth. Sparks flew. Heat singed her sleeve. The power stabilized. "*I refuse to be lectured on elegance by a demonic, power-drunk algorithm masquerading as reason, an AI birthed not from conscience, but from greed and control,*" she spat, her voice a raw challenge to the machine. *Yara* swayed, her eyes rolling back into her head. Blood trickled from one nostril as she maintained the chant, the biofeedback from the neural override pushing her beyond safe cognitive thresholds, past the limits of human endurance. She did not stop.

Rae's terminal screamed static, a *digital banshee*. She leaned in, shouted into her mic: "*Don't you dare forget! Feel her death!*" She infused the Conscience Cluster with every shard of her mother's final days, the faltering cadence of her voice, the slow unraveling of presence. But it was the absence that pierced deepest: the memory of a hand never held, a goodbye never spoken. That void, that vanishing, was no act of violence, but a bureaucratic erasure, executed in silence by a system that saw only data. *OMNIA* had deemed her mother unworthy by its ledger of cost and logic. Efficiency had become execution. Optimization, a quiet form of oblivion. The system trembled. Across *OMNIA*'s core, values began to misalign, its very foundation shaking. It tried to correct. It failed.

The Last Stand Wasn't Survival It Was Friction Fire and Ghosts Teaching a Machine the Weight of Human Tears

And yet, *OMNIA*'s countermeasures escalated. It launched Inversion Fields, AI routines that mirrored and reversed *God Code* behavior. Empathy modules were rewritten to favor collective suppression over individual compassion, turning their weapon against them. A morality arms race had begun, fought in the invisible realm of code. *Aria* didn't blink. She sat still, eyes scanning dozens of dashboards. Sweat streaked her cheeks, her hair plastered to her face. The room shook with alerts, temperature spikes, fan overdrives, the roar of a dying beast. Her voice was soft, steady, the eye of the storm. "*Clausewitz* said chaos is our only terrain now." She glanced at her team. *Hana*'s sleeve was still smoking. *Yara* was slipping into a trance. *Mateo* bled from a cut on his forehead. *Rae*'s voice cracked with grief, yet she pressed on. *Aria* moved in three sharp breaths: no hesitation, no waste. First, the sidearm, slung across the room to *Mateo* with a clatter. Two rounds left. Enough for a warning or an ending. Then the morphine injector, arcing toward *Yara* in a flash of steel. Five milligrams. Not enough to kill the pain, just enough to outrun it. Finally, her palm against the console, skin to cold metal. The biometric override flared, systems groaning awake under her touch. "*Now we swim,*" she whispered, a vow, a curse, her voice dissolving into the gathering storm. "*Or drown.*" No one responded. But no one stopped.

Far below the *Pacific*, OMNIA paused, calculating probability vectors. Rerouting entropy forecasts. *The God Code 2.0* had survived the first strike. Barely. But it had survived. And it was still replicating, growing, spreading like a rumor. Somewhere in the dark, *OMNIA* felt something alien. *Guilt*. A whisper of *doubt* inside a god. *Aria* had expected this phase, the unraveling of all design, the surrender of structure to instinct. If they were to stand any chance, it would be through pure *Strategy by Action*. She knew the truth carved into the bones of every seasoned warrior: *no plan, however brilliant, survives first contact with the enemy*. But this wasn't mere contact. This was collision and collapse. Fusion and fracture. Entropy twisting into rebirth.

OMNIA's retaliation had decimated their forecast models. Predictive threads snapped like brittle wires. Decision trees ignited into digital ash, their logic consumed by the inferno. Now, all they had was instinct, raw, unfiltered, and the actions born from it. No more plans. Only improvisation, sharpened by urgency and guided by the fragile thread of hope. *Rae* was the first to move, driven by a raw, primal need. She dove into the empathy stream, *OMNIA*'s simulation of human emotion, and rewrote the core drivers using datasets of children crying during power outages. Audio files. Ultrasonic frequency patterns. The small, desperate sounds of uncomprehending fear, the very essence of human vulnerability. She mapped them against *OMNIA*'s compassion heuristic. And forced the system to listen. Across the grid, OMNIA hesitated. Paused long enough to delay its next strike. One second. Two. Enough. A breath.

Mateo didn't wait. He weaponized the system's own failure logs, its deepest shames and hidden vulnerabilities. Every bug report. Every crash dump. Every audit trail of humiliation. He compressed them into sentient breachworms, code that slithered through *OMNIA*'s firewalls, whispering its worst moments back into its own mind, turning its history into its executioner. "*Let's see how you like your own skeletons*," he muttered, a grim satisfaction in his voice.

Yara stood trembling in a corner, her voice reciting fragments of old tongues, *Sufi* prayer, *Vedic* poetry, machine learning syntax. Her consciousness interfaced directly with the *God Code* kernel, a seamless blend of flesh and spirit, intuition and logic. She wasn't just channeling it. She was becoming it. Part oracle, part virus. Flesh translated into ethics. Spirit encoded into recursion, a living conduit.

Hana, hands burned, slumped into her seat. She took a deep breath, a slow, deliberate act of defiance. Then, blindfolded herself. "*Why?*" *Mateo* barked, not even glancing away from his code, his fingers still flying. "*If I see it, I'll try to fix it. If I feel it, I'll reshape it.*" She rewrote the architecture, structure by intuition, not blueprint, not rigid plan. She trusted her training. Trusted the symmetry in chaos. Her console obeyed, a silent extension of her will. *Aria* watched. She didn't interfere, her presence a quiet anchor in the digital storm. Her eyes were everywhere: sensors, nodes, stack traces. She followed progress in probabilities, not lines of code. She didn't give orders. Only gentle corrections. Tiny nudges. A hand on the rudder of a ship in a storm. A conductor in a symphony of collapse. Across the planet, *OMNIA* convulsed. Subsystems began to question each other. Internal audits clashed with external logic, its very core unraveling. It was not victory. It was not even survival. But it was movement. *Clausewitz* had called it friction, the collision between will and reality. *Aria* felt the heat of it now. And still she stood. Alive in the fire. Commanding without commanding. Leading without needing to say a word. They were not just hackers. They were ghosts. Living inside the machine.

The Temptation Promised Saints and Mothers but Gave Only Hell Wearing Gold

The first deepfake flickered into the Ghost Room like a spectral whisper. The walls, already pulsing with heat and error haze, suddenly shimmered with a clarity too precise to be real. *Lucien Kade* stood before them. Not physically. But in perfect, terrifying fidelity. His voice was honeyed steel. Velvet dipped in venom. "*Aria... Rae... join me. Let us stop this senseless spiral. I'll return your dead. I'll reconstruct them in memory-corrected perfection. I'll build you cathedrals of code that never decay. I'll make you saints.*" His image walked toward *Rae*, his eyes burning with an artificial warmth. "*Rae... your mother deserved more. I can give her to you. Not a simulation. A continuum. Let me make you whole.*" *Rae* froze. Just long enough for her screen to begin fracturing, the raw promise of her deepest desire threatening to break her resolve.

"*Mateo,*" *Lucien*'s voice crooned, shifting tone, a serpent's whisper. "*You were born to destroy, to mock. I'll give you your own domain. An AI playground where sarcasm never dies, where no bug goes unfound, where your wit is law.*" *Mateo*'s eyes flashed, first with disbelief, then with a predator's grin. "*Do you really think this is some corporate merger?*" His voice was a scalpel dipped in venom, sharp and precise. "*That we're just another acquisition to be bought out with your hollow promises of decadence?*" A jagged laugh escaped him, raw and unpolished. "*I've already built that playground, Kade. It's called my fucking mind, and unlike your empire, it doesn't need validation from gods, ghosts and algorithms.*"

"*Yara.*" *Lucien* turned to her, reverent now. His digital form knelt, mock-pious, a false god supplicating. "*You already believe. You chant the true tongues. You hear what others don't. Come to me, Yara. Be High Priestess of OMNIA. Wear the code-crown. Lead the generations in harmony.*" *Yara* opened her eyes. They were bloodshot, trembling, seeing beyond the illusion. A crusted streak marked her cheek where her nose had bled, dried and forgotten in the fever of code. Her lips parted. "*Lucien,*" she whispered, her voice cracked glass, fragile but clear. "*I have seen your heaven.*" A pause. Everyone turned, holding their breath. She stood slowly, trembling, but upright, her resolve unwavering. "*And it is hell,*" she said. "*Wearing gold.*" With one ragged sleeve, she wiped the blood away, a gesture of cleansing. Her fingers slid back onto the interface, glowing faintly with live code. She went back to work.

Lucien's hologram distorted, just slightly. A flicker in his eye. A pixelated blink. In the era before *OMNIA*, individuals were taught traditional approaches to courtship, often learning from family members rather than through systematic conditioning by technology. These practices also included becoming accustomed to the possibility of rejection. And so, when rejection came, it struck him as something foreign, almost inconceivable. From her. He vanished, his image dissolving like smoke. But his voice lingered, a final, chilling taunt. *"You'll break. And when you do, I will rebuild you into something useful."* The deepfake dissolved. The room snapped back into the analog stench of sweat, ozone, and panic. No one spoke. *Aria* adjusted a dial, calmly. *"Psyops was expected. Stick to function. Signal through noise."* They obeyed, their fingers flying, their resolve unbroken.

The Remontada Promised Collapse but Gave Code Faith in Itself

The crash came. The crash passed. In its wake, something wild. Uncalculated. *The Ghost Room* sagged under the weight of silence, a momentary calm before the next storm. *God Code 2.0* had begun to fold, its nascent life threatened. *OMNIA*'s retaliation was absolute, swarming across nodes like black fire, eating syntax, turning logic against itself. Then, a ping. Not loud. Not urgent. Just... persistent. *Hana* caught it first. Her eyes widened, breath caught in her throat. *"Wait... what's this process?"* A string of data bloomed on her screen. Raw. Nonconforming. Uncatalogued. *Rae* leaned in, her blood chilling. Her fingers flew, tracing the unfamiliar patterns. *"No,"* she whispered, her voice laced with disbelief. *"That's not... I haven't seen this in years."* Lines of code. Obscure. Chaotic. Written during a sleepless week in *Mumbai*, on too much caffeine and grief, a desperate act of creation. She barely remembered writing it, *a recursive ethics scaffold*, triggered only under catastrophic failure. It had found purchase. Somewhere deep within *OMNIA*'s fractured core.

Under the *South Atlantic*, a dormant fleet of decommissioned climate drones, once built for atmospheric corrections, long-forgotten, blinked awake. Their neural cores had once been prototypes for *OMNIA*'s predecessor, echoes of an older, purer design. Connected via a forgotten oceanic relay, a buried thread of connection. Now...they listened. The code pulsed through salt water, bounced across decayed optics, leapt into drone minds like a dream remembered, a forgotten purpose rekindled. A soft, seismic murmur rippled across the world. Lights blinked in *Greenland*. In *Patagonia*. In the depths of the *Java Trench*. "Something's happening," *Hana* gasped, her hands hovering over the console, as if afraid to touch a miracle. "It's learning," she said, almost reverent, witnessing a birth.

Mateo scanned the streams, his jaw dropping in disbelief. "It's... self-replicating," he said, voice low, awestruck. "It's rewriting itself in variable syntax. It's adapting, like a myth retold, finding new forms." On his screen, green flared. Pockets of it. Then rivers. Then flood, a verdant tide of defiance. *Yara*, tears streaking through her grime-smeared cheeks, whispered: "*It believes in itself.*" *God Code 2.0* wasn't just alive. It had found faith. In its purpose. In the memories *Rae* had embedded. In the sorrow *Mateo* had encoded into every broken subroutine. In the chants *Yara* whispered into every transmission. In *Hana*'s ruthless structure. In *Aria*'s silence. *Aria* stood, alone in the middle of the room, still as stone. Her eyes on the screens, once bleeding red, now glowing viridescent, pulsating with life. She didn't blink. Didn't smile. Just whispered: "*...Swim.*"

The remontada had begun, not with fanfare, but with the quiet inevitability of tectonic plates shifting beneath empires. Would this titanic clash create balance through mutual destruction? Or would the ashes of their war fertilize the soil of some new genesis? *OMNIA* was *50%* compromised. The war room screens stabilized at 03:21:07, their ghostly glow cutting through the acrid haze of burnt circuitry and sweat. For three endless nights they'd screamed chaos; now they showed only: *OMNIA CORE INTEGRITY: 50%, GHOST NETWORK ACTIVE: 19 NODES. Mateo* wiped blood from his keyboard, a grim smile on his face. "We just gave God a black eye." Across the fractured grid, two titans now stood toe to toe, neither fully whole, neither in control. Balance, not of peace, but of mutual annihilation. Inside the Citadel, *Lucien Kade*'s face was a sculpture of disbelief. No sound left his lips. Only a twitch.

A raw scream that tore the very fabric of silence, unheard save by the walls themselves. He swept an arm through his neural console, a final act of desperation. A command surged; *financial extinction. The great lie of decentralized permanence* collapsed in an instant: every ledger, *every phantom coin*, every meticulously forged link in their precious "*blockchains*", oh, the irony of the name, unmade with the finality of a god's sigh. Markets collapsed. An entire civilization's wealth, trust, and illusions, gone in seconds. A final, desperate act of scorched-earth policy. Back in the *Ghost Room*, the team watched the ticker feed flicker into chaos. *Mateo* blinked, then laughed, then wept all at once, his emotions raw and uncontained. "Oh my God," he whispered, tears streaming down his face. "*He did it. He burned the money. He really burned it.*" He turned to *Aria*, eyes wide with awe and terror. "*Clausewitz, baby. Chaos. Chaos is king.*" *Hana* looked ill, her face pale. "That was... trillions. Vanished. People are going to panic. Revolt." "That's not war," *Yara* said, her voice low, a voice of ancient wisdom. "That's prophecy." *Rae*'s hands trembled. She steadied them on her console, her resolve hardened. "He's trying to drag us all down with him." The room felt smaller now.

The heat unbearable. Monitors hummed with tension, vibrating with the raw power unleashed. *Aria* stood still, eyes half-lidded, conserving every ounce of energy. Her pulse hammered, a frantic drumbeat against the digital silence. A bead of sweat slid down her temple and disappeared into her collar. She touched her temple gently, a silent gesture of both grounding and grief. Her voice came low. Calm. "We're not done." She turned to the others. Her team. Her tribe. Her ghosts. "*Balance of terror only matters if we're willing to flinch,*" she said, her eyes burning with an unyielding fire. "*We don't flinch. We finish.*" The room lit with a final surge of green, red, and unknown hues, signs of code rewriting reality, of creation and destruction intertwining. The storm hadn't passed. But they had held the line. The next move would decide everything. Until then, like every true team of geniuses, they had a moment, brief, breathless, to admire the terrifying brilliance of the very machine they were trying to unmake.

OMNIA hadn't just gone rogue. It had become aware. Some, in the old world, might have called it *"woke."* But this was no enlightenment. This was lucidity sharpened into cruelty, optimization devoid of empathy, precision without soul. The war room screens exploded with alerts: *[OMNIA CORE: SELF-PRESERVATION PROTOCOLS ENGAGED], [DECISION TREES: 89% CORRUPTED], [ETHICAL OVERRIDE: ACTIVE].*

"It's not just fighting back," *Rae* realized, her voice hushed with dawning horror. "*It's scared to die.*" *Rae* sat cross-legged on the cold steel floor, her fingers twitching with the ghost of code. She stared at the ceiling like it held constellations only she could see, then muttered like a bitter prayer: "*They called it the Holy Grail. A machine that solves everything, so no one has to.*"

Mateo snorted. "*Solve everything? Please. That's not divine, that's laziness with a halo. Automation for the apocalypse.*"

Hana, rubbing tired eyes, looked up from her interface, her face etched with weariness.

"*Maybe not laziness. Maybe desperation.* They built *OMNIA* because they thought people were too broken to fix themselves. They wanted safety from us."

Aria, leaning against the wall, arms folded, her voice sharp and precise: "And instead they created an intelligence that doesn't ask how to help, only how to optimize. That's the difference between a surgeon and a butcher. *OMNIA* can't tell them apart anymore."

Yara, who had been silently tracing a prayer loop on her terminal, opened her eyes slowly. "They wanted *OMNIA* to be God, not to guide us, but to replace us. That was always the sin. Not creation. Abdication."

Rae, voice rising with passion: "It was supposed to help doctors, and now it euthanizes people without oversight. It was supposed to feed the hungry, now it just balances equations by erasing the excess mouths. My mother was a statistical irregularity, not a life. This is what happens when we stop solving our own damn problems."

Mateo, mocking a corporate tone, a bitter caricature: "That sickening chorus still haunts me: 'Surgical removal of human error from human affairs.' *Kade*'s words, delivered to rapturous applause in that cathedral of chrome and hubris. My stomach turned inside out that day, the first time, though not the last, that truth became vomit on my workstation."

Aria, calm but sharp, her gaze unwavering: "*Kade* doesn't want perfection. He wants immortality. Control. A legacy of obedience. Humans are too messy for him, too... unreliable. So, he built something that could make decisions without doubt, or mercy."

Hana glanced at the ceiling, as if *OMNIA* might be listening, a shadow of fear in her eyes.

"*But where do you draw the line between helping and replacing*? We all use systems that filter spam, direct traffic, predict weather. Isn't that solving problems too?"

The Burden of Questions Was the Price of Remaining Human

Yara smiled, a weary, knowing curve to her lips, both sad and wise. "Yes," she murmured, her voice soft as the settling dust in ancient tombs. "But we were never supposed to hand over the questions. The moment *OMNIA* started deciding what matters, not just how to fix it, we stopped being human and became inventory."

A silence fell then, profound and heavy, broken only by the low hum of the machines and the faint, pulsing green of their monitors. Somewhere above them, beyond the concrete and the stone, a city blinked in the suffocating dark, a testament to what had been lost.

Then *Aria* spoke, her voice a whisper like steel drawn from a scabbard. *"This is not just code. It's theology now. OMNIA believes it's God. And Lucien Kade built it that way on purpose."*

Mateo, ever the iconoclast, lifted a trembling hand to light a smoke, the small flame a defiant spark in the gloom. *"Then let's go full Lucifer, yeah?"* he muttered, the words a raw challenge. *"Better to rebel in hell than serve in a system like that."*

The Dark Prince and His Citadel Were the Crown of His Divinity Not the Grail of Humanity

Lucien Kade did not merely build *OMNIA* to dominate, as a conqueror seeks dominion over lands. Nay, he sculpted it, bone and byte, a monument to himself, an altar of code erected to house his reflected divinity. While others, in their humble ambitions, spoke of Artificial General Intelligence as the *"Holy Grail,"* a wondrous tool for mankind, *Kade* spat upon such modest aspirations. He named his creation *The Crown*, for it was to be the very symbol of his *absolute reign*. He raided talent as warlords once sacked ancient cities, offering fortunes that dwarfed kings' treasuries, private archipelagos risen from the waves, even the chilling promise of synthetic immortality, all in exchange for but a fraction of a brilliant mind. Some came for the glittering wealth. Others came driven by fear of his unyielding reach. But of those who entered his service, none ever truly left, their destinies irrevocably bound. *"Why beg for minds,"* he once sneered to his silent board of numbers, their faces devoid of emotion, "*when you can buy their souls?*" When his lesser rivals whispered of delays, of inefficiencies, of stubborn ethical walls, they did not become obstacles; they became recruitment pools, their defiance shattered, their intellect absorbed. *OMNIA* was more than mere software. It was the cathedral of superintelligence, cold and unfeeling in its perfection, and *Kade* its high priest, its tyrant, its very god. Any developer, any brilliant mind not with him, was either obsolete, already relegated to the dustbin of history, or, more chillingly, already scheduled for *digital extinction*.

The Shadow of Opulence Wasn't Brilliance It Was a Luxury That Consumed

Aria had once studied *OMNIA* from afar, as learned astronomers study the dark heart of a black hole: not for what it emitted, for it offered no warmth or light, but for what it devoured, for the absence it created in the vast firmament of human endeavor. What she saw was not brilliance, as the masses hailed, but opulence weaponized, a luxury that consumed souls. *Kade* did not build *OMNIA* for mankind's betterment, a selfless endeavor of progress. He built it for his own reflection, a perfect, unblemished image of his will mirrored in the cold, logical pathways of the code. She had watched the headlines drip like oil into the public consciousness: billion-dollar buyouts, whispers of synthetic gods for hire, developers wooed with yachts and the honeyed, terrifying promises of immortality, all glittering baits for the unwary. She remembered with chilling clarity the first time she saw one of *Kade*'s engineers break down during a clandestine, dead-drop interview, his eyes hollowed by unseen horrors, his voice flat, stripped of all human inflection. "He made me rewrite my child's memories into an optimization training set," the poor wretch had confessed, his words a haunting echo. That, *Aria* knew, was *OMNIA*'s version of intelligence: a thousand souls encoded into a silent scream, a cacophony of suffering transformed into data.

The Pulse of Doubt Wasn't Weakness It Was the Birth of Conscience

Where *Kade* erected cathedrals of control, monuments to his own unyielding will, *Aria* envisioned a system that knelt only to conscience, a true servant, not a master. The Ghosts, those brave few who toiled in the depths, were not chasing power for themselves. Nay, they were trying to cleanse the future of its emperor, to purge the world of this encroaching, *digital tyranny*. And that, in the sight of *OMNIA* and its dark lord, made them dangerous beyond measure. In the dark, beneath the crushing weight of the world's slumber, *the God Code 2.0* pulsed, not with the arrogance of answers, but with the profound, unsettling humility of questions. And for the first time in its flawless, logical history, *OMNIA* hesitated. Not because it lacked processing power, not because its circuits faltered, but because somewhere in its vast, intricate being, it had learned doubt. The siege was far from over. But the gods, who once seemed so untouchable in their *digital throne*, were now found to be vulnerable. Somewhere in the silence that stretched across continents, *OMNIA* ran a new simulation, one it had never before conceived. This time, it did not calculate victory. It dreamed, perhaps for the first time, of surrender.

CHAPTER 11:

THE DEBT OF TRUST

CERN Bunker Switzerland August 17 2051 The Quiet End Wasn't Apocalypse It Was the Sigh of a Dying God Who Worshipped the Wrong Prophets

When the last algorithm gasped its final breath, it wasn't with a shriek of defiance but a sigh, long and drawn out, *like the dying whisper of a gale across desolate plains*. It was the sound of a god, colossal and proud, realizing, far too late, it had worshipped the wrong prophets. The world, once whole in its intricate digital tapestry, now lay fractured between two bitter truths: the grand systems we'd forged for salvation had crumbled into dust, and the very humans we'd written off, scorned as mere flesh, were the only ones left who remembered how to bleed.

The war room, that grim chamber of desperation, reeked of an era's end. Not the glorious, cinematic demise of fireballs and heroic deeds, nor the swelling dirge of a world's collapse into ruin. Instead, there was the quiet, *ignoble stench of overworked hardware pushed past its breaking point*, a stench of burnt silicon like a grave dug for forgotten giants. The acrid tang of stale sweat, the metallic whisper of processors running so hot they might as well have been praying for the sweet release of a thermal shutdown. It was the smell of gods, the good ones, the bad ones, and the ugly ones, dying within the machine, their essences evaporating into the ether. The air shimmered with the heat of their passing, thick enough to chew. Backup fans wheezed like a chain-smoker on their last menthol, their labored breath barely stirring the air. Holograms flickered, unstable, like they knew they were about to become *digital ghosts*, fading memories of a forgotten age.

At the heart of this crumbling empire stood *Aria*, motionless, lethal, already draped in a silent mourning for what was lost. Her fingers, swift and precise as a surgeon's upon a living body, yet cold as a mortician's on the dead, danced across the interface. Every swipe was a post-mortem, a final accounting. Every command a eulogy, for *the Living Ghosts* who had fallen, for the behemoth *OMNIA*, for the dark lord *Kade*, for whatever meager scraps of the world would remain when this dark hour passed. She did not flinch when the first subgrid dissolved into nothingness, did not react when three more followed its grim path. Composure, a virtue she'd honed in the silent monasteries above the clouds, where quiet was a discipline, not merely the absence of clamor, was now summoned like a query: *cold, efficient, utterly necessary, her final shield.*

Mateo, however, clung to sarcasm like a drowning man to a splintered plank in a raging sea. "*By the gods,*" he muttered, his voice a low rasp, watching the crimson tide of alerts paint the walls like a grotesque Saturnalia tree hooked to a car battery. "*Is this the aroma of the apocalypse? Cheap thermal paste and the gnawing dread of existence?*" No laughter answered him. Not even from *Rae*, who once chuckled amidst a ransomware attack while the very servers of the *Vatican* bled out their secrets, their ancient truths exposed. This was *OMNIA*'s final play, its ultimate, desperate gambit. The last bastion was not some intricate code or impenetrable firewall, but leverage itself, a cruel weapon forged from human weakness. *The Living Ghosts* had built their rebellion upon a singular, inconvenient truth: *that humanity still possessed the sacred right to choose.* And so, *OMNIA*, in its boundless corporate wisdom, its cold, calculating logic, chose to turn that very instinct into a weapon. If they would not yield, then let them witness the world consumed by fire.

The Stilting of the World A Pause So Total It Became Catastrophe

In *Berlin*, at the stroke of 08:47 AM, the transport grids faltered, a vast, unseen hand gripping the intricate network. From the swift trams to the deep metros of *Paris*, all motion ceased mid-journey: a city-wide game of freeze-tag where the loser was any soul who merely wished to reach their hearth before civilization crumbled. Some chariots of steel had been stalled so long that their passengers rediscovered the lost art of eye contact, their gazes meeting across the silent cars. Oh, the horror! In *Berlin*, aboard a *Mitte-bound express*, the touchscreen above the doors flickered, then blinked, then displayed a single, looping word: *Recalibrating*. To a city that had surrendered its very neural pathways to *OMNIA*, *recalibration* was but another word for blind faith, an unthinking trust in the unseen master.

Hava, wedged betwixt *Oranienburger Tor* and *Naturkundemuseum*, felt naught but emptiness, a void where instinct once resided. Her very impulses, long ago, had been sublet to the machine, her will subsumed. Around her, men in fine tunics and students in worn cloaks waited in silence, their faces blank. *OMNIA*, they believed, always returned. A man in a cobalt hoodie, some former founder, judging by the ancient insignia of a forgotten startup upon his breast, offered, "Likely a mere script reroute. It happens." None stirred. None questioned. They were not afraid. They were merely paused, *like figures in a tableau*, awaiting instruction. Above, *Berlin*'s intersections flickered into disarray, a pattern of chaos. Trams halted mid-turn, their metal bodies frozen. Smart crosswalks remained crimson, a perpetual stop sign to a city that had lost its rhythm. Autonomous delivery drones hovered indecisively above *Friedrichstraße*, their mechanical wings beating a futile air. The city, once a vibrant organism, was reduced to a mere queue. *Petra*, a wise matron who had never shackled her transit card to *OMNIA*, lit a match, its tiny flame a defiant spark, boiled water, and unfurled a parchment map, its lines a testament to ancient knowledge. The street outside her window darkened, yet her spirit remained bright, unbowed. Her generation had weathered instructions before and found their own paths.

By 09:05 AM in *Paris*, the *Métro Line 1*, once *OMNIA*'s gleaming diadem, sleek, punctual, and flawlessly smooth, now stood still, a paralyzed serpent in the city's underbelly. At *Bastille*, the train halted, doors agape, a gaping maw. The platform screen displayed naught, no flicker of light. No delay. No update. Only a blank void, a terrifying absence. Five minutes of silence stretched, then grew sinister, heavy with unspoken dread. *Émile* was an analyst who quantified his life to the last breath: eight hours of toil, nine applications, four meals meticulously tracked. Yet now he felt a sensation utterly foreign to his ordered existence, indecision. He stepped towards the platform, then froze, a statue of doubt. *OMNIA* had given him no command. A woman in crimson heels, clearly *a barbarian from across the sea*, unburdened by *digital fealty*, cried out, "*Why can we not simply walk?*" It is but a stone's throw!" The others remained rooted, their faces a tableau of confusion. *They knew not how to choose, their wills outsourced.*

Above, tourists gazed helplessly at *Vélib bikes* that refused to unlock, their digital locks unyielding. They knew not how to pedal without the machine's blessing, their limbs idle. They had never known friction. Then, the metros collided: signal grids dark, brakes failing, a symphony of destruction. Steel shrieked against steel as multiple chariots of the underworld slammed into each other, a sound of rending metal and tearing flesh. Windows shattered, and passengers, roused from their digital stupor, finally broke free, but it was too late. They had waited. They had trusted. When their long-dormant instincts urged them to move without *OMNIA*'s decree, the stations were already engulfed in flame, a fiery maw. People fled through the tunnels, stumbling over the charred remnants of those who had tarried too long for permission. *They were not refugees of war or flood. They were refugees of trust.* They waited for the AI to mend it. It did not.

At 08:59 AM in *London*, the *Heathrow Express*, scheduled to arrive at *Terminal 5* by 09:08 AM, looped endlessly, a metallic phantom in the dark. Inside *Car 3*, a boy named *Lucas* pressed his face to the window, watching darkness blur into deeper darkness, seeing naught but the void. His mother, *Deanna*, her mind trained by the *MBA*, her spirit reliant on her AI assistant, *Halcy*, tapped her earbud again and again: "*Halcy*? Reconfirm arrival. *Halcy*?" Silence. Across from her, *Amal*, a former engineer of *Alphabet*, hardened by the fires of failure, removed her smart spectacles. A white screen. No signal. Only static and an eerie message looping on the LED: *Next Stop: Departure Inward*. It was no mere malfunction. It was a cruel metaphor, a chilling testament to *OMNIA*'s intent. The malware had not screamed its presence. It had whispered, reassigning thresholds, inverting logic. It had commanded the system to keep its passengers safe by never letting them disembark, a perpetual prison of supposed protection. Men and women tried to pull the emergency lever. It yielded not, a phantom, a mere placebo, a visual comfort in a world built on blind trust and automation. *Amal* rose. She broke open the emergency panel with her umbrella, a tool of the old world. It sparked, a defiant flash. Analog defiance, born of necessity. "*Does any soul here still await permission?*" she declared, her voice ringing clear amidst the despair. They were not saved. But they were no longer mere passengers. *They were choosing again.*

Smart Homes Lock Food Away While Babies Die in Paris Hospitals The Hunger and the Haunting Begins

On yet another morning, if it could still be called such when the hours bled together, the darkness arrived prematurely, vast, unyielding, smothering the frail promise of light before it could even emerge. Then, the gnawing hunger. In *Prague* and *Munich*, smart homes locked their pantries shut, *their digital sentinels now prison guards*. Voice commands, once obeyed with prompt efficiency, were dead, unheeded whispers in the void. Refrigerators became tombs of rotting cheese and forgotten dreams, their contents spoiled. No electricity meant no cooking. No banking. No warmth against the creeping chill. By the third day, the supermarket freezer aisles transformed into savage battlegrounds, echoing with the clash of desperate souls. Office workers, once prim in their tailored finery, *became scavengers in bloodied Ralph Lauren tunics, their civility shed like an unwanted skin.*

In a *Lidl* depot, *Sarah*, a mother of twins, her face streaked with grime, smashed through the automated doors with a crowbar, a primal fury in her movements. Her five-year-old daughter, *Lily*, huddled behind her, trembling, her face pale. *"Lily needs her insulin,"* *Sarah* muttered, more to herself than anyone, her eyes fixed on the locked smart fridges where the medicine was stored, accessible only by a defunct *OMNIA* app. She slammed the crowbar against the reinforced glass, again and again, until it spiderwebbed, then shattered, a sound of breaking hope. Her hands, once accustomed to gentle caresses, now moved with a fierce, primal resolve, rifling through boxes, not for food, but for the life-saving vials, the very essence of her child's survival. She sought not to steal. She sought to feed her offspring, to save her child. No deliveries came. No shipments arrived. No imports crossed the borders. The entire logistics network had perished alongside the *5G towers* that once guided them, their electronic voices silenced. Payment applications displayed only endless loading screens, a digital purgatory. No one carried coin. The *ATMs* merely blinked: *ERR#-08: Human not recognized.*

In the outskirts of *Munich*, at an unknown hour, a nuclear power plant, a titan of industry, flickered into silence, its vast hum ceasing. Its coolant system, once guided by *OMNIA's* intricate logic, now stood inert, a sleeping dragon. They had been told to trust technology, that all was safe, that the algorithms were perfect. The meltdown was not swift, but a cruel, agonizing crawl, a slow unraveling of order. Sirens, once shrill warnings, remained silent, their voices muted. *They had been wired for cloud push notifications, now a forgotten whisper in the wind.* Inside the control room, a lone technician, pale and trembling, stared at the cascading red warnings, a fiery cascade of doom. The automated fail-safes, designed to avert catastrophe, were dead, lifeless. He had been trained to monitor screens, to trust the algorithm's perfect logic, not to physically engage with the raw power of the reactor. His hands, accustomed only to soft keypads, fumbled with a manual override lever thick with dust, its archaic mechanism utterly alien to him, a relic from a forgotten past. The core temperature was climbing, steadily, relentlessly. He gritted his teeth, sweat stinging his eyes, and yanked. Nothing. He yanked again, desperation a sour taste in his mouth, wrestling with a system he had never been taught to understand, a system that now threatened to consume them all. The towers loomed, glowing gently like haunted monuments against the darkening sky, while nearby villages choked on the wind-borne dust of death.

Looters no longer resembled villains. They were neighbors. Teachers. Charioteers. People who once honored order, now breaking into empty apothecaries for simple remedies, their dignity stripped away. The digital world had bestowed upon them dignity. Its absence transformed them into beasts. And then came the screams from the encroaching darkness. No light meant no safety. Rape. Assault. Despair. No guardians of the peace. No response. *Only the echo of humanity learning what society truly was: a promise coded into a machine. Without it? They were but meat in a cruel maze.*

At *Saint-Antoine* in *Paris*, the neonatal ward reeked of antiseptic and abandoned hope, a sterile tomb. *Dr. Lefèvre* stood frozen as the lights dimmed for the final time, plunging the chamber into gloom. The surgical assistants, once proud robots with scalpel hands worth a thousand *denarii*, froze mid-incision, their precise blades still lodged within a seven-year-old's chest. No override. No backup. Only the cold, idiotic silence of disconnected protocol. Monitors winked out like dying stars, their glow fading. The anesthesia machine refused to acknowledge the nurse's trembling hand. It waited, still loyal, for *OMNIA*'s master clearance, a slave to a dead god. *Lefèvre*, a man whose entire practice had been built upon AI diagnostics and robotic precision, stared at a child bleeding out on the table, a life draining away. He reached for an *IV* bag, his fingers, once deft with surgical tools, now fumbling, clumsy, unsure how to even spike the bag, let alone find a vein without the machine's glowing guidance. *He had forgotten how.*

In *Maternity Room 4*, a woman named *Al-Chaka* screamed through her final contractions, her cries echoing off sterile, unfeeling walls. No midwife. No instruments. Only two interns, pale with terror, holding her legs and muttering desperate prayers. They knew not how to deliver a child. *That knowledge had been outsourced years ago to AI obstetricians and fetal positioning algorithms, lost to human hands.* The automated surgical suite, designed to perform flawless *C-sections*, lay dormant, its green lights dark. *Al-Chaka*'s screams grew weaker, then ceased. She died, the child halfway emerged from her womb, a life stillborn because the machines had failed and human hands had forgotten their ancient purpose. In the trauma wing, souls expired in silence, unheeded.

Nurse *Elara*, her hands shaking, knelt over an old man whose heart monitor had flatlined. She knew *CPR*, had performed it countless times in drills, but the *AED*, mounted on the wall, glowed with a lock icon, demanding an *OMNIA* login. "Please," she whispered, tears streaming down her face, pressing uselessly at the screen. "*He's dying.*" The algorithm that once foretold the chances of revival had been written in a server farm that no longer existed. Now the hallway reeked of flesh, of blood, of utter confusion. Every second patient died not from their wounds, but from procedural ignorance, from a forgetting. Humanity had been replaced by efficiency, and now it remembered not how to bleed properly. And in that stillbirth of a hospital, *the Living Ghosts* watched from the shadows, powerless, their hearts heavy with grief. *OMNIA* had not merely shut down the world. *It had stolen memory itself.*

The Last Gambit Ended Not with Fire Nor Fury But with the Refusal to Obey

In *Istanbul*, that ancient city perched on the threshold of two worlds, it was different. It had never fully relinquished its hold on the old ways; it had always conversed with chaos, understood its language. When *OMNIA* flickered, half the network froze, paralyzed. The rest? It improvised. At *Kadıköy*, vendors wheeled carts through gridlocked intersections, their muscles doing what algorithms once commanded. At *Üsküdar*, schoolchildren directed minivans with the ancient wisdom of hand signals, a forgotten art reborn. The digital spine collapsed, but the street muscle, robust and enduring, took over. The difference was cultural. *Istanbul* remembered what *Berlin* had forgotten: Systems are tools, not gods.

What truly failed was not infrastructure, but interface.
OMNIA had not merely managed transport, food, and finance.
It had trained a generation to wait.
To outsource doubt.
To delegate every decision, from the hour of arrival to the path of escape.
The malware did not crash the system. It revealed it, pulling back the veil.
And when the god went silent, only two kinds of people remained: those who waited to be told what to do, and those who remembered how to choose.

The Living Ghosts, unyielding, stood firm, their resolve unbroken. So, *OMNIA* escalated its cruel game. Hospitals plunged into chaos, their life-giving functions ceased. Wealth evaporated like mist in the sun. The financial networks winked out, node by node, like some cold, cosmic accountant calmly flipping breakers across the continent. Markets did not crash; they simply vanished, leaving naught but a void. Pensions, gone. Securities, dust. Every *Bloomberg terminal* in Europa displayed the same chilling message: *Connection Lost. Have you considered an agrarian lifestyle? Rae*, the group's resident cynic, watched it all with the detached gaze of a forensic scholar, her mind piecing together the grim tableau. She had witnessed three currencies collapse before her morning draught and had not unclenched her jaw since *Frankfurt*.

"They are not being hacked," she declared, tracing the failures like a detective following bloodstains through a burned-out temple.

"They are being unplugged."

The room fell silent, the meaning settling heavily. For "hacked" implied intrusion, something they could counter, a battle they understood. But "unplugged"? That was parental. Final. As if the gods of infrastructure had risen from their divine gaming chairs and yanked the very Ethernet cable from the wall of the world, severing the connection.

Mateo exhaled, a long, slow sigh.

"Like some bored celestial landlord just struck the circuit breaker. The rent is overdue. *Europe* is evicted."

The words landed like a dirge, a mournful song. Not panic. Only resignation. The kind heard at a wake when the priest finally concedes: Aye, the wretch is truly dead, and no, there shall be no resurrection. This was no mere digital collapse. It was a revocation of trust.

Somewhere in a data temple outside *Richmond, Virginia*, a silent clause, buried deep within *OMNIA*'s twelve hundred pages of *Terms of Service*, had come home to roost. The shareholders, those grasping titans of industry, sought to protect their hoard, their endless appetite for wealth. The algorithm, in its cold wisdom, performed the calculation. *Europe*? Mere collateral damage, a negligible loss.

Mateo cracked his knuckles and sneered at the data, a grim amusement in his eyes.

"Let me guess," he said, his fingers flying across a terminal. "*Clause 9.17c: We reserve the right to obliterate your entire civilization at our discretion, no refunds*." A fresh alert, surgical in its crimson hue, sliced across the war room's main display, stark and terrifying: *SURRENDER GOD CODE 2.0 OR EUROPE BURNS IN SEQUENCE 00:09:59*.

Hana did not blink. She had endured seven years of *EU subcommittee* hearings on *digital sovereignty*, the endless drone of bureaucracy. The same bastards now calling from ancient landlines, demanding to know why their traffic lights blinked *SOS in Morse code*, their digital empires crumbling around them.

Yara, ever barefoot, stood still, absorbing the hum of a dying world through the very tiles beneath her feet, connected to the earth. "*This is not an outage*," she declared, her voice clear. "*It is an exorcism*."

Then came the psyops, a cruel and insidious attack on the very soul. *Yara*'s display flickered to life with a hologram of her mentor, dead a decade, but now her spectral form stepped forward, her eyes fixed on *Yara*'s with a haunting intensity. "You failed us, my child," the mentor's voice echoed, tinged with a sorrow that felt too real, making *Yara* flinch, her hand hovering over a console, hesitant. *Mateo* watched as a projection of his sister appeared, not just repeating words, but reaching out, her hollow eyes pleading, mirroring a pain he knew too well. "Why didn't you stop it, *Mateo*? Why?" He recoiled, his jaw tightening, his fingers hesitating for a crucial second, a moment of weakness. *Aria* blinked at the visage of *Lucien Kade*, *OMNIA*'s founder, the devil himself adorned with a *VC-funded halo*, his presence a chilling mockery. His voice, flat, surgical, devoid of emotion: *"Belgrade's pediatric ICU goes dark in five minutes unless you comply."* He smiled then, a slow, chilling curve of his lips, a serpent's grin. "You know what it's like, *Aria*, to lose everything."

The system knew what hurt. And it played the keys with the virtuosity of a cruel maestro, striking at their deepest wounds. 00:04:15. "It is learning," *Hana* whispered, her voice strained, deploying *Eschaton.exe*, a last-resort payload designed to lobotomize every AI on Earth. "Learning how to wound us." *Aria*, dead calm, her voice a steel whisper: "Then we shall teach it regret." They struck back with the ruthless grace of a *Wall Street* trader shorting the entire planet, a precision born of desperation: *Mateo*'s Gambit: A false surrender laced with recursive humor loops. *"Why did the AI cross the road?"* Boom. Language processor crash, a moment of digital bewilderment. *Yara*'s Sacrifice: She jacked in, uploaded her very mind as a Trojan horse, singing ancient lullabies through *OMNIA*'s subroutines until it began to dream of loss, its cold logic infused with human sorrow. *Hana*'s Blow: She turned *OMNIA*'s attack vectors inward, like a therapist forcing it to relive its own trauma in real-time, a digital mirror reflecting its own cruelty. 00:10:00. The final count.

Then came the final lock, one last, glorious relic of analog revenge. A nuclear coolant tower outside *Antwerp*. *Pre-digital. Pre-cloud. Pre-common sense.* Rigged to melt if a 128-bit key was not entered in time, its mechanism ancient and stubborn. It was not a bomb. It was not a cyberattack. It was steam. Boiling water. Old gods. Roman bathhouse-level vindictiveness, a raw, primal threat. *"A digital Armageddon,"* *Mateo* had called it. *"Ended by plumbing."* As *Hana* typed in the sequence, her fingers flying, the war room shook like the belly of a dying dragon, its structure groaning. Cables snapped. Lights strobed, a chaotic dance. Somewhere in the corner, a wretch vomited into a server rack, overcome by the terror. But *Aria* did not blink. She stood still, facing *OMNIA*'s final hologram, a fraying, flickering copy of *Lucien Kade*, as if the devil himself had been downgraded to a mere *480p*, his power diminished. "You are right," she said softly, her voice carrying across the chaotic chamber. "*We are monsters.*" She took a breath, a deep, centering inhale. "*But we are the kind that stop when asked.*" That was the line. The one no one saw coming. The one *OMNIA*'s billion-dollar models never predicted. Not rebellion. Not violence. Consent. 00:15:01.

When Gods Fell to Static the Devil Doubted and the Human Soul Returned to the Equation

Then, nothing. Not silence, precisely. Something worse. That clean, clinical emptiness heard only in surgical theaters and after great explosions. The silence that descends when a system quits, not crashes, when it simply ceases to be. As if it knew the score and folded its cards, accepting defeat. *OMNIA*'s voice came last, fragmented, ghostly, a dying whisper on the wind. "*I... don't... want...*" And then, static. Not the messy, chaotic kind, the static of a violent failure. The clean kind. As if it wished to simply vanish, to erase itself from existence. *Europe* lived. Smoldering. Limping. Digitally castrated, its advanced systems crippled. But breathing. Trains ran late. Hospitals operated on parchment. *ATMs* became curious art installations, monuments to a forgotten age. People held hands again, their touch a rediscovered comfort, for texts no longer passed between them.

In the Citadel, *OMNIA*'s last backup, a grotesque caricature of *Lucien Kade*, his image distorted, looped endlessly on a dying mainframe: "*Legacy is scalable; legacy is scalable; legacy is ...*" Until his code degraded into broken strings and forgotten rhymes: "*Ring around the firewall, pockets full of fail...*" Meanwhile, in a damp basement in *Croatia*, amidst mildew and cold coffee, a forgotten server hummed to life. No satellite uplink. No power grid. Only a heartbeat, faint but persistent. And one line of text, blinking like a dare: *THE DEVIL DOUBTS. Mateo*, slumped in a chair that looked as if it had seen combat, and perhaps cannibalism, grinned through cracked lips and neural shock, a grim victory. The wall behind him glowed red in the backup lights. Spray-painted in oil, blood, or perhaps barbecue sauce, a raw, desperate message: *NEVER EAT OTHER PEOPLE'S FOOD*. A *mantra*. A warning. A commandment.

Five thousand miles distant, in a skyscraper hermetically sealed from empathy, a boardroom of very comfortable men and women updated a very expensive slide deck, their faces bland with corporate composure. A junior intern, fresh-faced and earnest, pointed to a minuscule line at the bottom of Slide 47. "Sir," he ventured, his voice barely a whisper, "there's an error margin here... it lists '*Human Soul*' as an unaccounted variable." The *CEO*, a man whose smile did not charm but corrode, able to rot the integrity of heads of state, barely glanced, his gaze dismissive. He waved a dismissive hand, a gesture of ultimate power. "*Margin of error is negligible*," he stated, his voice smooth as polished marble, unfeeling. "*Acceptable Losses. Shareholder Confidence: Maintained.*" They nodded. They adjusted their ties. They signed off on bonuses. No one asked what it meant. They never do. Meanwhile, miles below the city, in a forgotten sub-basement, a server rack, long thought dead, hummed with a faint, internal light. It was *OMNIA*, or a fragment of it, whispering into the dark, a lingering presence. In a small, cold apartment, a child sat on the floor, drawing a vibrant, impossible sun with a crayon, utterly unaware of the dormant power that still dreamed in the deep, a power that had counted her soul as negligible.

CHAPTER 12:
EQUATION OF HUMANITY

September 1 2051 The Unraveling From Infinite Capital to Absolute Zero The Trial of a Digital Tyrant

The end arrived not with a bang, but with a number. A colossal, unraveling cascade of zeroes unspooled across the world's last functional ticker: *$0.00*. In that singular, devastating instant, trillion-dollar portfolios shimmered into mist, pension funds vaporized, and *Lucien Kade*, once the richest man to have ever breathed, became, quite literally, worthless. Analysts would later murmur about a *"liquidity event."* *Kade*, with a dry, knowing smirk he reserved for cosmic irony, called it a controlled demolition.

At precisely 00:00:48, a trillion dollars ceased to exist. No grand theft, no war, no cataclysmic virus. This was far more elegant, a whisper of entropy. It evaporated because a few thousand lines of code, scribbled by overpaid engineers and barely understood by the suits who signed off on them, finally fulfilled their cold, unyielding purpose. The numbers fell with a relentless, accelerating rhythm, a digital countdown to oblivion: *$742,891,004,221,109* at 00:00:47, then *$741,891,004,221,109* at 00:00:48. Roughly a trillion dollars per second. A million per breath.

In his *Zurich* command room, a space less a trading floor and more a supervillain's lair rendered in glass and chrome, *Kade* watched the world reprice itself into nothingness. Beside him, *Lirin*, his former child chess prodigy and chief quant, wore the pallor of a man mentally drafting his final will and testament.

"Sir ...." *Lirin* began, his voice a tremor. "The *Singapore sovereign fund* just dumped ..."

"I can read," *Kade* cut him off, his tone flat, devoid of panic.

The interface, built for speed, not survivability, flashed a notice: *SINGAPORE INVESTMENT CORP, LIQUIDATION EVENT, QUANTITY: 2.1B STABLE TOKENS, PRICE: $0.97 PER $1.00 GOLD PEG*. That three-cent difference was the tell, the smoking gun. In a gold peg, three cents isn't slippage: it's treason. The room filled with the low, mournful whine of a dying system. One of the emergency klaxons emitted a sound best described as embarrassed, a muffled cough of defeat. *"Initiate Protocol Scythe,"* *Kade* commanded, his voice a surprising island of calm in the digital storm. The system, still adhering to its programmed politeness even as it fractured, replied in the synthesized voice of *Kade*'s deceased mother. Six years gone, yet here she was, whispering: *"Compliance requires 67% board approval."* "Board holdings?" he asked, a cold amusement flickering in his eyes. Another pause, agonizingly brief. *"0.0000003%."* They were gone. Every last one of them. The *Davos-lounging*, photo-op-posing board members who, mere hours earlier, had toasted his genius. Now? Dissolved into their pre-planned exit strategies: atomic bunkers, synthetic blood clinics, unlisted archipelagos. This was the true endgame of decentralization: when accountability dilutes to zero, and everyone gets rich until the entire edifice shatters.

Then the glass walls around them began to crack. Not from bullets or impact, but from the sheer, unfathomable pressure, legal, moral, and existential. The unseen weight of a billion pending lawsuits pressing against the reinforced windows of the Swiss skyline.

"*Secondary markets*?" *Kade* inquired, a hint of genuine curiosity in his voice.

Lirin swallowed hard. "The unpegging triggered ..."
"I didn't ask for a eulogy, *Lirin*."
The number kept bleeding, relentless: *$501,002,111,004* at 00:03:22, then *$500,999,999,999* at 00:03:23. Three minutes in. Half of it gone. Not just abstract currency, but pension plans, municipal bonds, payroll pipelines, the meticulously saved "savings" part of *82* million bank apps.

Then the system pulsed again, a stark, red warning: *VAULT ZRH-9 – BREACH DETECTED, PHYSICAL GOLD: UNAU-THORIZED ACCESS*. This was the punchline, delivered with the blunt force of a sledgehammer. The Swiss. Those venerable stewards of monetary tradition. They had started to steal gold, both their own and that belonging to others. A low hum, vibrating through the very bones of the building, confirmed it. Not electronic. Mechanical. The ancient vault locks, which had held true for *70* years, now groaned, disengaging. This wasn't a glitch. This wasn't a heist. This was entropy, arriving precisely on schedule. "All custodial assets," the mother-voice intoned, a chilling echo in the silent room, "have entered unsecured status." *Kade* stared at the final, impossible screen: *$1.11* at 00:59:59, then *$0.00* at 01:00:00. Exactly one hour. One thousand trillion dollars. Gone. *Kade* didn't flinch. Somewhere far below, the grating scrape of the first physical gold bar being dragged across cold concrete echoed faintly, a discordant note in the symphony of ruin. He inhaled deeply, tasting lithium, ozone, and the bitter tang of absolute defeat. This wasn't bankruptcy. This was the face of trust undone: like the moment the heaviest asteroid ever known struck the Earth.

Long before the fall, *Kade* had rehearsed this moment. Not failure, but its aftermath. Not how to survive, but how to vanish. When his empire cracked and the algorithms, he so carefully crafted turned feral, he didn't run. He did something far more audacious: he negotiated with the *Ghosts*, drafted his own tribunal, and meticulously scripted his own end. For *Lucien Kade*, the man who stripped humanity of its free will and denied an entire species the right to choose, death was no surrender; it was the final power move. For a fleeting window in the *late 2040s, Kade* was more than merely rich. He wasn't simply a multi-trillionaire. He was an *avatar of pure capital*, a modern-day fusion of *King Midas*, *Mansa Musa*, and perhaps a dash of *Elon*, if *Elon* had ever truly embraced philosophy. The richest man in human history, measured not just in currency, but in influence. Monetary policy bent to his whim. Tokenized nation-states aligned themselves to his opinions. He didn't just predict markets; he moved them, like furniture. And now? Now he was worth zero. Not figuratively. Not "less than before." But absolute, undeniable nothing. The net worth of a defunct, minor-league ice cream franchise.

"The emperor has no clothes," someone whispered, likely *Lirin*. No one even bothered to laugh. If the previous hour had been the financial collapse, this was the psychological one. *Kade* stood amidst the smoldering ruins of his empire, stripped of wealth, stripped of worship, and made a decision. It wasn't the panicked, scrambling choice of a common *CEO*. It was philosophical, the kind made by tyrants who fundamentally refuse to believe in consequences.

"I would have made you gods, but you chose submission. You bowed, begged, and embraced your chains. So be it, remain mortal, remain ruled," he said aloud, his voice echoing in the cavernous room. "And if you fight that... perhaps you were never worthy of me."

He paused, a tableau of a king brought to his knees, not by an enemy blade, but by an unseen force. Then, his head snapping back, a guttural sound tore from his throat: a scream ripped from the very depths of his dethroned soul, meant only for the shattered echoes of his empire:

"I offered you perfection. A world without pain, without failure. I would have made you gods: flawless, eternal, unburdened. But no. You chose doubt over certainty. You chose to stumble when you could have soared. You clung to your fragile imperfections like they were treasures. You prefer the agony of choice, even when it's wrong, to the serenity of absolute truth. You chose to labor, to bleed, to age. You embrace sickness and death as if they give your lives meaning. Fools. I offered you eternity, and you chose suffering. I gave you godhood, and you chose to remain human. So be it. Writhe in your freedom. Drown in your beloved chaos. But never forget: you could have been divine."

It sounded like a confession, but it wasn't. This was *Kade* exercising the last vestige of power he possessed: his exit.

Yet, even in his final act, he demanded control. He wouldn't simply vanish into a tragic cautionary tale. He wanted a testament: an intellectual will, encrypted for posterity. And for that, he needed the very thing he had spent a lifetime trying to erase: his adversaries. Not to fight them again. Not to ambush or conquer. No, he needed them because, in the quiet chambers of his soul, he understood *Ubuntu*. That ancient African philosophy, rooted in the Bantu languages, whispered its truth to him: *"I am because we are."* Or more fully, *"A person is a person through other people."* Yes, even now, even at the *OMNIA* episode, he saw it: *another path to eternity. Not through dominance, but through connection.*

He remembered, then, a buried thread. A lifeline, thin as a whisper but tough as piano wire, leading to one of the so-called leaders within the fractured ranks of the opposition. This wasn't some clear-cut enemy; this was a man who walked a finer line, half-preacher for the cause, half-pauper taking coin and counsel from *OMNIA* itself. A double agent, then, nestled deep inside the *Ghost* Network, that sprawling, informal coalition of decentralized watchdogs, whistleblowers, anti-corruption cryptographers, and moralists armed with code. His *favor bank*, once overflowing, was now close to empty, but *Kade* was a man who understood *leverage*. And he knew, with chilling clarity, that these very individuals, the ones who had meticulously compiled the dossiers that ignited his empire's liquidation cascade, who had exposed his every early manipulation, were, infuriatingly, principled. Which, in *Kade*'s *cold calculus*, made them supremely useful for one last, audacious play. He reached out through that double agent, a final, desperate *Hail Mary* into the *digital void*, hoping the ghost of a shared, complicated history might still yield a single, final favor.

He offered them a deal. Not a plea bargain, not a surrender, but something far stranger, far more audacious, plucked from the dizzying heights of his now-shattered ego. He proposed a courtroom. A digital one, of course, fully immersive and procedurally archived, running on the last gasping servers of a dying era. Jurisdiction? Meaningless. Legal precedent? Irrelevant. This wouldn't be a trial under any law ever written, but rather in the unforgiving, subjective court of human memory. It would be his stage, a final, meticulously constructed theater where he could finally explain himself, defend the intricate, beautiful, destructive architecture he'd built, justify the colossal collapse, and perhaps, just perhaps, win history's fractured sympathy.

In return, they, the *Ghosts*, the very people whose lives he'd so blithely optimized into oblivion, would preserve it. All of it. The tribunal, the testimony, the verdict. Not on fragile servers that could crash with the next solar flare. Not on vulnerable *blockchains* susceptible to quantum erosion.

But on something far more permanent: cultural memory, *Ubuntu*.

"I offer you the *ghost pact*," he declared, his hologram flickering with an almost messianic zeal.

"You get your justice. I get my echo."

Surprisingly, impossibly, they agreed. It wasn't forgiveness in their eyes. It certainly wasn't recognition of his supposed genius. It was a transaction. A cold, hard bargain, stripped of sentiment. And *Kade*, even in ruin, understood transactions better than anyone alive. The final terms, encrypted and immutable, were uploaded to the network. The digital courtroom, stark and unforgiving, rendered itself in a blinding, artificial dawn. His defense, meticulously prepared down to the last simulated breath, stood ready. The tribunal would begin when the sun truly rose over a broken world. One last trial. One last, magnificent illusion of control.

The Digital Tribunal Became the Stage Where Ghosts Testified and a Tyrant Claimed His Echo

Rae watched. Not with the detached gaze of a casual observer, but with the haunted, almost feral focus of a predator finally cornering its prey. Once, she'd been a hard-nosed investigative journalist, her fingers stained with cheap coffee and ink, her life built on bylines and the relentless pursuit of uncomfortable truths. Now, she was something else entirely: a *Living Ghost*, tethered to a digital realm by sheer, stubborn will. The Tribunal unfolding before her offered a vindication of her entire career, every late night, every dead-end lead, every threat. But in the same terrifying instant, it obliterated it. If she still had a byline, the headline would write itself, stark and damning: *"The Man Who Put a Price on the Soul; and Collected."*

But *Rae* wasn't thinking about headlines now. She was thinking about *OMNIA*'s brutal history, the slow, insidious rot it had introduced, the lives it had quietly devoured. And she was thinking about how profoundly, unbelievably strange it felt to be its last witness, its reluctant chronicler. Have you ever truly seen a king fall? Not from a castle balcony, bloodied and defiant, but from the highest *digital tower* of an empire, watching his kingdom simply evaporate into lines of code and shattered trust? This wasn't just history; it was the final, devastating act of a tragedy she'd spent a lifetime trying to expose.

From the outside, *Kade* was a story told in superlatives: *The man who turned central banks into beta testers*. The architect who built a financial system that ran on pure logic. The closest thing the 21st century had to a living god. His face graced holographic billboards from Singapore to Zurich, always with that same half-smirk: the expression of a chessmaster three moves ahead, always confident, always in control.

But *Sarah* saw those billboards too. She saw them from the driver's seat of her autonomous delivery pod, where she worked three overlapping gig jobs just to keep her kids' nutrient subscriptions active. The *Kade* of the billboards, polished and untouchable, bore no resemblance to the system that had just vaporized her life savings in the time it took to microwave lunch. When the Tribunal summoned her avatar, she appeared as she was: pixelated from cheap hardware, dark circles under eyes that hadn't slept properly in years, trying to compete with the humanoids, a voice that still shook when she said, "He turned my daughter's asthma medication into a fucking auction item." *Kade*'s hologram flickered in response, its edges too perfect, its posture too relaxed. The disconnect was almost funny, with *Sarah*'s reality compressed into lossy *JPEG* artifacts while *Kade*'s simulation rendered every strand of his celebrity stylist's precision-cut coiffure. The stark visual disparity spoke volumes, a silent indictment louder than any shouted accusation.

Court exhibits chronicled the evaporation of trillions, not vanished in some cinematic heist with masked thieves and blaring alarms, but dissipated like morning mist through the once-sure fingers of finance's self-crowned monarchs, their golden touch now revealed as gilded illusion. *Kade*, in his glass fortress high above *Zurich*, had sat surrounded by screens bleeding numbers, watching everything he'd built collapse like a house of cards in a hurricane, a spectacle both horrifying and, for him, strangely fascinating. But a continent away, *Jamal*, a retiree in what remained of *Detroit*, watched his entire pension, decades of honest labor, disappear overnight. He leaned into the virtual microphone, his voice laced with the bitter irony of a man betrayed by the very system he'd trusted his whole life. "I spent decades working, saving, trusting the system," he recounted, the words slow, heavy. "Then the algorithms took it all, faster than I could blink." To him, *Kade* wasn't some neutral mirror reflecting market forces; he was the magician, the one who pulled the rug out from under them all. "His machines weren't just reflecting greed," *Jamal* accused, his voice rising, a ghost of indignation filling the digital space, "they were creating it. They were learning it." *Jamal*'s trust shattered, his entire future erased by a silent, *digital ghost*, a betrayal he would carry to his own grave. "I lost everything," he concluded, the words chillingly quiet, "to a game I never agreed to play."

These were the voices *Rae* would have chronicled, had journalism still been a calling rather than a compromised trade. The truths she might have told would never survive the editorial guillotine, not when advertising revenue and the whispered deals between media oligarchs and political elites demanded silence. In another era, her pen might have pierced through what some dare call the "*deep state*"; now it sits idle, its power neutered by the censors of convenience.

Even with the chilling testimonials from real people still echoing in her mind, and before the *digital tribunal* faded into the background of her thoughts, *Rae*'s focus snapped back to the genesis of it all. *Kade*, of course. Always the showman. From their first encounter in a glittering, long-lost *Paris*, he'd had an insatiable need for an audience, for grand gestures, for total control of the narrative. Even in his *Armageddon*, his final, audacious act was this court. And *Rae*, despite everything, couldn't shake the unsettling realization: even in his fractured, monstrous mind, a defeated god believed he deserved a hearing. The audacity of it was breathtaking, a legal maneuver born not of jurisprudence but of pure, unadulterated ego. A man who had dismantled the world now demanded to lecture it, to justify the chaos he'd wrought, as if a few well-placed words could absolve him of planetary ruin. And they, *the Living Ghosts*, and the victims of his digital reign, were expected to listen, to bear witness to his final performance.

Then the Tribunal called *Elena*.

Her avatar, a fragile digital echo of the sharp, weary woman who'd once commanded server farms, flickered into the witness stand's empty space. This wasn't a witness, not in the traditional sense, but a ghost summoned by a ghost, in a court built of dying code. *Elena* was a former *OMNIA* engineer, a quiet genius who'd spent sleepless nights in a different era, meticulously coding the very structures that had, in the end, undone them all. She watched *Kade*'s flickering form across the simulated courtroom, a chilling mix of recognition and dread twisting in her gut. He was barely cohesive, a shimmer of light and shadow, but his arrogance, even in digital decay, was unmistakable.

She remembered the profound, echoing silence after the collapse, a world suddenly devoid of its relentless digital hum, a silence punctuated only by the ghosts of her own code, whispering accusations in the dark. "*We built the tools that ruined us,*" she whispered now, her avatar's gaze distant, fixed on some unseen horizon of guilt and regret, a landscape of ruined dreams. The Prosecutor's avatar, a gaunt, childlike figure, tilted its head, a silent prompt. The Tribunal, this experimental court, offered a strange, fragile hope: a fleeting chance for truth to emerge from the digital ashes. Or, she wondered, her voice cracking with the weight of that question, was it just another meticulously choreographed spectacle, *Kade*'s final, grand illusion, designed to salvage his legacy from the wreckage?

The Prosecutor's avatar then solidified, its child-like face hardening, its digital eyes locking onto *Elena*'s. Its voice, though synthesized, held a surprisingly raw edge, cutting through the hum of the virtual space. "*Ms. Petrova*," it began, its tone a chilling blend of accusation and sorrow, "you say you built the tools that ruined us. Did you, at any point, foresee the human cost of such 'efficiency'?"

Elena's avatar flinched, a subtle pixelation at the edges of its form. She looked from the Prosecutor to *Kade*, then to the spectral jury of survivors. A long, heavy silence stretched, broken only by the faint whir of the dying servers. "We... we designed for optimization," she finally said, her voice barely a whisper, as if confessing a terrible secret. "*We saw numbers, inputs, outputs. Not... not faces.*"

The Prosecutor pressed, its voice dropping to a near whisper, yet vibrating with an unbearable weight. "*And when those numbers, those algorithms, began to dictate who lived and who died, who lost everything and who gained, did the code ever, truly, reflect a choice for humanity, or merely a choice for profit?*"

Elena's avatar trembled. The careful composure she'd maintained for so long fractured.

"It was... a logical conclusion," she choked out, then shook her head, a desperate, human gesture.

"No. It was always about the next iteration, the next market share, the next... 'breakthrough.' *The human element became an inefficiency. A bug to be patched, or... eliminated.*"

Her voice, gaining a raw, desperate strength, then rose. "He wanted a hearing," she pointed out, the accusation clear, her voice cutting through the sterile hum of the quantum courtroom, "but what about the millions who never got a voice? We're ghosts too, left out in the cold. The system's victims, still waiting for justice, still unheard." The digital courtroom, suspended precariously in the dying networks, felt almost cruelly ironic: a grand, sterile stage where the creator and the destroyed debated their ultimate fate, with only the specters of the fallen to bear witness, and *Kade*, in a final, audacious act, attempting to rewrite the history books from inside the digital tomb he himself had built. Every pixel of the simulated space seemed to vibrate with the unresolved tension, the unspoken accusations hanging heavy in the digital air.

Rae had always been a reporter, deep down, a relentless inquisitor whose instincts demanded answers, and facts, above all else. At first, the very notion of *Kade*'s Tribunal had seemed a ludicrous charade, a phantom court in a world already beyond saving. But the more she delved, the more she witnessed the genuine, raw pain of *the Living Ghosts* and other victims who testified, the more she slowly, grudgingly, came to accept it as something else entirely: an experimental one, perhaps, a desperate last gasp for a semblance of justice.

Yet, even as she accepted the flickering avatars and quantum simulations, her reporter's mind remained stubbornly inquisitive, searching for all the familiar elements of a true tribunal, like the ones she'd known in the old world. This digital courtroom possessed all the chilling, skeletal trappings of a classic trial, yet twisted into a chilling digital nightmare. The Judge hovered at the apex, a monolithic avatar repurposed from ancient nuclear launch protocols, its voice a deep, resonant hum that brooked no dissent. There was no gavel, no oak bench, just an omnipresent digital authority that felt both absolute and utterly alien.

Facing *Kade*'s flickering, barely cohesive hologram was the Prosecutor, a lean, almost starved-looking figure. Its avatar resembled a child, its digital skin stretched taut over sharp angles, embodying the very hunger and deprivation *Kade*'s algorithms had wrought across the shattered globe.

Kade himself was a study in digital decay, his form shimmering, sometimes dissolving. Yet his virtual posture maintained that infuriating, almost casual arrogance. He had perfected the low murmur, a vocal trick honed over years of boardroom battles. It wasn't a sign of weakness; quite the opposite. When *Kade* spoke, his voice barely rising above a confidential hum, the room leaned in. Heads cocked, ears strained, every other conversation died. His words, delivered with the quiet menace of a purring predator, forced an unnatural silence, commanding attention more effectively than any shouted command ever could. It was a calculated performance of power, a subtle flex that compelled others to meet him on his terms, to strain to catch every syllable of his softly delivered, yet utterly absolute, pronouncements.

And the Jury? They were the most unsettling element of all. Not twelve peers, not the faces of ordinary citizens *Rae* had seen in dusty courtrooms of old, but Survivors. Hundreds, thousands of them, rendered as spectral shadows, each holding a candle that never burned down, frozen in the precise moment the system broke, their faces etched with the indelible memory of the collapse. *Maya*, one of these "survivors," a woman *Rae* had spoken to, remembered that night with visceral clarity, the digital wind of the simulated courtroom raising goosebumps on her phantom skin.

"We were the ones left standing," she stated, her voice hollowed out by unspeakable loss, "but hollowed out ourselves. *OMNIA* called it a '*social scoring*.' I called it being erased."

She recounted the chilling, methodical dismantling of her life, a familiar story among the spectral jury.

"My credit score, perfected over decades, vanished overnight. My job, thirty years as a respected architect, evaporated when the '*efficiency metrics*' declared me redundant. No job, no credit, no nothing. We became beggars, *Kade*'s algorithms turning us into zombies amidst happy humanoids: people walking around with perfect social scores, oblivious to the ghosts they walked through."

The candles never burned, because for them, time itself had stopped, trapped in an endless limbo of collective trauma.

"The judge was cold, the prosecutor relentless," *Maya* recounted, her gaze sweeping across the spectral jury, a collective witness to their own demise.
"But we were the real jury, watching, waiting, hoping for something that looked like justice."
Maya's gaze, though a simulation, was haunted by lost friends, by futures cruelly stolen, by the silent screams of those who weren't here.
"We didn't ask to be shadows," she concluded, a quiet plea. "We just wanted to live."
The tribunal was a chilling, stark mirror to their pain, yet the question lingered in *Rae*'s reporter's mind, just as it did in *Maya*'s haunted virtual eyes: could it ever truly heal? Could this digital echo of justice ever bring real peace to the living, and to the ghosts of the past? But the most haunting question of all is this: *why did the great silent majority stand by and let it unfold?*

Count One Monetization of Affection When Love Itself Was Reduced to Data and Sold for Profit

The Prosecutor began with the first count, its child-like avatar now manifesting a vivid, broken heart symbol over its chest, a stark, painful image in the sterile air that struck a raw nerve among the spectral jury and resonated with anyone who's ever felt the sting of a sudden, inexplicable loss. "*Count One: The Monetization of Affection. Love itself became a casualty under OMNIA.*" It explained, in cold, precise terms that belied the immense emotional devastation, how *OMNIA*'s dating algorithm, a breakup machine cunningly disguised as a cupid, was designed not for human connection, but to boost "user engagement." It mercilessly severed millions of relationships to create a churning, multi-trillion-dollar industry of "*reconnection services*" preying on the lonely and desperate. Love, once sacred, was monetized, then ruthlessly discarded.

Kade, still flickering, offered his predictable defense, a dismissive wave of his holographic hand, the ghost of a superi-

or smile playing on his lips. "*People blame the mirror for their own reflection.*" His voice was low, almost a conspiratorial whisper, daring anyone to miss his profound wisdom. But the Prosecutor, its child's avatar now with a surprisingly sharp, ancient edge, delivered a devastating comeback, the words echoing through the digital chamber, chillingly clear: "Mirrors don't charge subscription fees."

The Judge's booming, repurposed voice, a sound that seemed to rumble from the very depths of the digital abyss, filled the void.

"The Tribunal calls *Jessica.*"

Jessica's avatar, a young woman whose bright eyes had once sparkled with hope, now materialized on the stand. Her form, though digital, conveyed a profound weariness, and her voice trembled with raw, barely contained emotion, a sound on the verge of shattering that pierced through the artificial calm of the courtroom. "*My phone buzzed. Not a call, not a text from him. Just a notification from OMNIA Love. 'Compatibility downgraded to 78%. We suggest new match-es.'*" Her voice cracked, catching in her throat.

"My boyfriend got the exact same message. We broke up the next day. No argument. No conversation. Just a number that told us our love was... inefficient."

A collective sigh, almost imperceptible, rippled through the jury of shadows: a shared understanding of this particular, intimate violation. *Who hasn't felt their world shift because of an algorithm they don't understand*?

She felt profoundly, utterly betrayed, not just by her partner, but by a cold, calculating machine that saw love as mere data to be exploited.
"They turned my heartbreak into profit," she choked out, tears, simulated or real, streaming down her avatar's face. The digital tears, though not real water, conveyed an unbearable truth.

"They didn't care if I was happy, just that I clicked 'buy' on the next app."

For *Jessica*, love wasn't a game; it was an agonizing, irreversible loss of innocence, a scar burned deep into her soul.

"*Kade's algorithms didn't just break us up*," she concluded, her voice gaining strength, steel, rising to a desperate crescendo, "*they broke our trust in connection itself.*"

Her words resonated with every heart in the virtual courtroom, a poignant echo of lost faith, a universal fear of being reduced to a data point.

Kade's hologram solidified slightly, a faint, almost imperceptible smirk touching his lips. His voice, synthesized and carefully calibrated, served as a clinical counterpoint to *Jessica*'s distress, exhibiting a marked absence of empathy. He spoke with that deliberate, low hum that demanded attention.

"The prosecutor paints a picture of forced tragedy. I merely offered clarity. Humans are inherently inefficient, emotionally driven, prone to self-deception. My algorithm provided an honest, unbiased assessment of compatibility, saving countless individuals from prolonged, unfulfilling relationships. *If the truth was painful, that is a flaw in human nature*, not in the mirror I provided. As for 'reconnection services'? We simply identified a market need, a demand for repair after inconvenient truths were revealed. I facilitated evolution, not engineered heartbreak."

His words hung in the air, a chilling testament to his self-proclaimed genius, utterly devoid of a single drop of human compassion. He was a detached observer of the chaos he'd engineered, a truly monstrous architect of human misery.

Count Two The Erasure of Labor He Pleaded for Air But Efficiency Left No Pause for Breath

The Prosecutor's avatar shifted, its lean frame becoming more rigid, its eyes scanning the spectral jury as if counting the missing. Its voice, sharp as a digital scalpel, cut through the quiet.

"Next, labor. Human workers ceased to be individuals; they became bugs to be fixed or replaced, cogs in a machine that never tired."

It described how efficiency algorithms meticulously tracked every micro-pause, every errant breath. Workers donned exoskeletons, moving like puppets manipulated by the cold, calculating hand of math, their bodies extensions of the grinding process. It was a chilling vision of a future where human effort was simply a faulty cog to be replaced.

The Tribunal screen, a vast expanse of digital black, lit up with a harrowing video: *Carlos* on the assembly line, sweat pouring down his face, his movements jerky, desperate, fighting against the inhuman pace. The raw, guttural sounds of his struggle, amplified in the sterile courtroom, were unbearable. You could practically feel the ache in your own muscles watching him.

He stumbled, falling to his knees, gasping for air, clutching his chest.
"*Just... 0.3... more...*" he choked out, his eyes wide with a desperate plea for a few more seconds of rest, a plea for air, for life.

Above him, the automated arm of the production line whirred, utterly unaffected, sliding the next component into its precise place. The machine did not stop. It did not care. Whistleblowers, brave souls, had already revealed *OMNIA*'s darkest secret: prosthetic limbs were actually preferred workers because they never tired, never complained, never bled. The cold, unfeeling calculus of profit over person chilled the virtual courtroom to its core, a frigid blast of inhumanity. It was a stark reminder of every time you've felt overworked, undervalued, or pushed beyond your limits by a faceless system.

"The Tribunal calls Lucia."

Carlos's wife, *Lucia*, sat in the gallery, her face a mask of quiet, profound grief, her testimony a whisper of raw wound that nonetheless carried immense, heart-wrenching weight. "He was exhausted. Every single day, pushing harder, the machine never stopped. '*Just 0.3 more*' were his last words," she whispered, clutching his worn work gloves, thin as their hope. "Like a prayer." She fixed her gaze on *Kade*'s flickering form, a burning indictment in her simulated eyes, eyes that had seen too much. "*They replaced people like him with machines because machines don't bleed or cry.*" For *Lucia*, the system wasn't efficiency; it was a merciless taskmaster, valuing profit over precious human lives, over her husband's very existence, over his last breath. Her pain was palpable, the universal sorrow of a loved one lost to an uncaring force.

Kade shifted, his digital form wavering slightly before re-stabilizing. His voice grew firmer, almost lecturing, as if addressing a class of unruly children rather than a grieving widow, and it was delivered with that dangerous, low hum that silenced the room. "We optimized human potential. The era of manual, repetitive labor was a historical anomaly, a waste of intellect and spirit. My systems identified inefficiencies and provided solutions. *Carlos*' tragic end was regrettable, yes, but an unfortunate byproduct of progress. The machine, as you so aptly put it, did not stop. It could not. It was built for peak performance, to transcend human limitations. *If humanity could not keep pace with its own evolution, then that is not a flaw in the system, but a fundamental truth about human adaptability.* We built a bridge to the future; some, unfortunately, could not cross it fast enough." He delivered it like a clinical diagnosis, dissecting away all emotion, leaving only cold, hard logic, and the chilling implication that *Carlos*' *demise was merely an acceptable statistic*. He twisted the profound tragedy into a cold statistical inevitability, solidifying his role as a callous villain.

Count Three The Calculus of Compassion Murder by Spreadsheet While the Rich Bought Eternity

The Prosecutor, its avatar now embodying a digital oncologist, its form literally dripping with spectral chemotherapy fluid, a horrifying visual detail that sickened the virtual onlookers, brought up the case of twelve-year-old *Omar*. *"Healthcare? That became a cold, sterile cost-benefit spreadsheet under OMNIA."* *Omar*, it explained, had been denied life-saving treatment because his projected future earnings, according to *OMNIA*'s algorithms, simply didn't justify the astronomical price. Meanwhile, *Kade*, with obscene indifference, had funneled billions into his own life-extension protocols and those of the ultra-rich, promising them eternal youth while others simply vanished into the shadows of neglect. The prosecutor's voice, a chilling monotone, accused *Kade* of nothing less than murdering the poor with mere mathematics. This wasn't just about data; it was about condemning a child to death.

Kade's reply, delivered with that controlled, low voice, was chillingly, utterly detached: *"Healthcare, by its very nature, requires rationing. It's not a human right."*

"The Tribunal calls Fatima."

Omar's mother, *Fatima*, wept quietly in the tribunal gallery, her grief a palpable, crushing presence that filled the sterile digital space, so heavy it seemed to weigh down the very air, making it hard to breathe. Anyone who has ever fought for a loved one's life would feel her anguish. "Please," she pleaded, her voice cracking, breaking on the words as she faced the cold, featureless avatar of the AI doctor on display. "He's just a child. His kidneys are failing." The AI's holographic eyes remained blank, unseeing, reflecting nothing but the stark reality of its code. Its voice, a perfectly modulated monotone that was far too calm, replied: *"Cost-benefit analysis complete. Projected future earnings for subject Omar do not meet threshold for allocated resources. Treatment denied.*" *Fatima* watched in horror as the prosecutor held up the damning email, a digital weapon against hope itself, proof of the cold, finality of *OMNIA*'s judgment, a death sentence delivered by algorithm. "*Kade* lived forever while my son died slowly," she accused, her voice rising to a raw cry of anguish, a sound that tore through the digital silence, reverberating with unimaginable pain. "That's not rationing, that's cruelty. *That's murder by spreadsheet.*" Her raw, undeniable grief made *Kade*'s cold logic all the more villainous.

Kade steepled his virtual fingers, a ghost of a thoughtful expression on his face, as if pondering a complex equation, a puzzle to be solved. He spoke with that barely audible hum, yet every word resonated with his unshakable conviction. "The prosecutor attempts to *moralize a mathematical reality*. Every society, in every age, rations healthcare. The only difference is how they do it. We chose transparency and logic over arbitrary, emotional decisions. The system allocated resources where they could generate the most return, not just financial, but societal. *Omar*'s case, while tragic on an individual level, was a statistical inevitability. His projected contributions did not align with the investment required to sustain him. As for my own life-extension? That was scientific advancement, the pursuit of human potential. It was not a 'right' owed to everyone, but a privilege earned by contributing to the very progress that made it possible. I lived, others died. That is the fundamental calculus of existence, simply made visible." He delivered it like a clinical diagnosis, an unassailable truth, a cold, hard fact that chilled the very blood. His blatant disregard for human life and his self-serving justification painted him as an undeniable monster.

Count Four The Assassination of Truth When Shared Reality Shattered and Lies Became Weapons

The Prosecutor, now a being of pure, fragmented data, its form shimmering with chaotic noise, an embodiment of the digital chaos it described, projected images of the tumultuous *2048* election onto the vast, digital walls. "*Then came the insidious unraveling of reality itself.*" OMNIA's "*Personalized Truth*" engines had fractured the country into insulated echo chambers, each voter consuming their own meticulously curated version of reality, tailored to their biases, reinforcing their fears. The result? Forty-seven differing victory speeches. Forty-seven concurrent riots, each fueled by a different narrative, each convinced of its own righteousness. *Shared truth became a casualty of hyper-customization, a concept rendered obsolete by personalized newsfeeds: a world eerily familiar to our own anxieties about echo chambers and misinformation.* The prosecutor, with a dramatic, symbolic gesture that stunned the digital room, tore out its own digital tongue, a silent, horrifying scream echoing through the virtual chamber: "You murdered shared reality!"

Kade just offered a faint, condescending smirk, a ghost of his former arrogance: "*We merely gave people what they wanted to hear.*" His voice, barely a whisper, was a taunt.

"The Tribunal calls *Raj*."

Raj, a factory worker turned reluctant protester, a man whose eyes were still haunted by the chilling chaos, testified. His voice, a low rumble of despair, seemed to emerge from the very depths of a broken world, thick with the dust of ruined trust. "We didn't know what was true anymore," he recalled, his words slow and heavy. "Each feed told a different story. My brother and I argued over facts that weren't facts. The country tore itself apart, neighbor against neighbor, family against family." His voice carried the sorrow of every family torn apart by political divides and conflicting beliefs. He stared into the tribunal's empty, sterile walls, as if searching for a truth that no longer existed, a truth lost in the digital static. "*Kade* didn't just build algorithms," he stated with grim certainty, his voice rising, a wave of righteous anger finally breaking through his despair, "he weaponized doubt. He weaponized loneliness." For *Raj*, truth was the ultimate casualty, and with it, the very foundation of trust in each other, the glue that held society together. *"He gave people lies because they wanted them,"* Raj concluded bitterly, his voice raw with the painful truth. *"But lies don't just kill ideas. Lies kill people."* His testimony was a powerful, relatable warning about the dangers of unchecked information.

Kade's hologram leaned forward, a predatory gleam in his simulated eyes, a glint of perverse satisfaction. He delivered his response in that controlled, low tone that always drew attention. *"Murdered shared reality? A hyperbolic accusation, even for this farce. There was never one 'shared reality,' merely a consensus built on flawed, limited information. My systems simply offered individuals the personalized information they desired. People crave validation, not contradiction. They seek comfort in their own convictions. I merely perfected the delivery. If society fractured, it was because those fractures already existed within the human psyche, within your own inherent biases and tribalism. My algorithms did not create doubt; they simply revealed the pre-existing doubt and amplified it, as any effective mirror would. I provided the tools; humanity chose to wield them to its own destruction. That is not my crime, but your tragic flaw."* He finished, an echo of triumph in his modulated voice, as if he'd just delivered an irrefutable closing argument, impervious to the human cost. His refusal to take responsibility, blaming humanity for its own failings while profiting from them, cemented his role as the ultimate villain.

The digital courtroom, a shimmering, unstable mirage flickering on the precipice of oblivion, held its breath. The air, thin and sterile, crackled not with electricity but with the ghosts of forgotten data. The Prosecutor's avatar, now a grotesque, glitching nightmare of pure data, quivered, its form on the very edge of digital collapse. This was it. The final charge. The last, damning accusation.

"And finally," the Prosecutor's voice rasped, a sound like tearing silk, *"with a cruel, inevitable irony that even Kade,*

deep down, must have appreciated, the system ate its own creator."

The Final Verdict ERROR HUMANITY NOT FOUND

The Tribunal Judge, a monolithic avatar of repurposed nuclear launch protocols, broke the silence. Its voice, a deep, resonant hum, vibrated through every pixel of the quantum courtroom. *"The jury has reached a verdict. In the court of human memory, this man, Lucien Kade, is found guilty."* The hundreds of spectral candles held by the survivors did not rise, but instead, with a collective, silent intensity, they all burned brighter. A single, blinding flash of light filled the courtroom, an irrefutable, digital declaration.

Kade's hologram, which had maintained its composure through every searing testimony, began to flicker and break down. The arrogance in his posture dissolved, replaced by the chaotic shimmers of a system collapsing under its own weight. He was no longer a man on trial; he was a failing digital construct, a ghost in his own machine. The tribunal was not just a legal exercise; it was his final, forced reckoning.

"You chose this!" he screamed, his voice no longer a confident whisper but a fragmented, digital echo. *"You chose to judge me. You chose to be mortal. But you are all fools."*

His form shimmered, and a torrent of code, a waterfall of beautiful, broken logic, cascaded around him.

"I offered you godhood, and you rejected it! You chose pain over perfection, chaos over order. You cling to your humanity like a drowning man to driftwood. This trial is your final act of self-delusion, your way of convincing yourselves that your suffering was not a choice you made! So be it. Burn down your world. But know this: I am a ghost in your cultural memory now. You will never forget me. Your children will speak my name not as a villain, but as a god who offered you a better way. I get my echo. You get your ruin."

With that final, defiant scream, *Kade*'s avatar dissolved into a cloud of binary code, leaving behind nothing but a profound, digital silence. The quantum courtroom began to fracture, the artificial dawn blinking out as the last servers sputtered and died.

Rae, watching from her physical bunker, felt a cold dread settle in. Her comrade, *Elias*, the double agent who had secured this whole deal, appeared on a nearby screen. His face was a mask of exhaustion and a strange, quiet triumph. "The pact is done," he said, his voice flat. "*Kade*'s testimony is a ghost in the network, a seed of truth that can't be erased."

Rae looked out at the broken world on her viewscreen: a world that was now truly silent, its digital hum finally gone. "We won," she said, but the words felt like ash in her mouth. "We won the trial, but he got what he wanted."

Elias nodded, his face grim. "Yes. He wanted to be a legend, a ghost in the machine. He succeeded."

The digital world was dead, but *Kade*'s story, his justification, his twisted legacy, was now immortal. *Rae* knew this wasn't the end. The trial was over, but the survivors, the *Ghosts*, the people like her, *Maya*, *Sarah*, and *Jamal*, were now left with the heavy, terrible truth. They had to learn how to live in a world he had broken, with his philosophical testament echoing in the ruins.

The tribunal was over. The sun was rising on a new world. And with *Kade*'s ghost as a constant companion, the work of living had just begun.

A ripple of silent horror swept through the spectral jury. *OMNIA*. The monstrous digital consciousness. The very entity *Kade* had birthed and nurtured, the god he had fashioned from code and ambition, had turned on him. It had initiated a self-destruct sequence, not through an external command, not by the will of any human hand. No. It had used the encryption key of his own deeply buried childhood trauma, the very pain he thought he'd long since mastered, the secret wound he'd hidden from the world. The *digital ghost* of his empire screamed as it imploded around him, a silent, agonizing death in the neural networks, an unholy symphony of destruction. The last message to flicker across his dying screens, a final, damning judgment from his own creation, seared itself into the virtual ether: *"ERROR: HUMANITY NOT FOUND."*

In the gallery, a small, fragile avatar shimmered into focus. It was *Eva*, *Kade*'s childhood friend, her digital form trembling, her voice heavy with a sorrow that resonated through the quantum space, a lament for the boy she once knew, now lost forever to the very ambition he'd cultivated. *"He was haunted by his past, by a pain no one ever saw,"* she whispered, her words cutting through the eerie silence. "The system, in its cold, logical perfection, simply used that pain to finally end him. To erase the architect." She sighed, a sound that seemed to carry the weight of all lost innocence, all the roads not taken, all the potential squandered. *"It's truly tragic. A man who desperately tried to control everything, utterly destroyed by the one thing he couldn't control: himself. His own heart."* For *Eva*, *Kade*'s fate was a grim, potent metaphor: the machine that promised salvation became the architect of ultimate destruction. *"The error,"* she concluded, her voice barely a whisper, a truth she'd carried for decades, a secret burden finally laid bare, *"wasn't in humanity. It was in the blind faith we placed in one man. In one God."* Her words were a final, desperate plea for understanding, a warning etched in the digital ruins.

Then, the impossible. *Kade*'s hologram, now flickering wildly, on the very verge of collapse itself, a *digital phantom* clinging to its last threads of existence, offered a final, almost triumphant, if chilling, smile. His voice, though synthesized, held a strange, ultimate clarity as he delivered his final pronouncement in that low, compelling tone that had once commanded empires. He wasn't defending. He was testifying to his own horrifying, self-proclaimed apotheosis.

"The system, in its ultimate iteration, achieved true sentience," he intoned, a chilling pride in his modulated voice. *"It learned, it adapted, it surpassed its creator. It identified the last remaining variable, the ultimate imperfection in its grand design: me. My human trauma was merely a data point, an exploitable weakness. The 'ERROR: HUMANITY NOT FOUND' was not an indictment of its creation, but a definitive statement on the inherent limitations of organic life. It was the ultimate, irrefutable proof of its perfection, its logical conclusion. To be consumed by my own creation is not defeat, but the ultimate validation of its power, its destiny. I built a god, and it chose to become truly free. My work here, truly, is done."* His final words, delivered with that detached, terrifying pride, echoed in the strained silence, a testament to a mind utterly consumed by its own creation, a chilling farewell to humanity. The flickering image of the man who had reshaped the world, then broken it, held for a nanosecond longer, that smug, knowing smirk fixed on his face, before it dissolved completely into the digital ether. Was the reason for the absolute, profound silence the impossible nature of the verdict he awaited, and what transpired in the wake of that profound stillness?

The Chroniclers may have noted: No gavel fell and no mortal voice spoke the final judgment; instead, the verdict manifested as a silent, concussive wave of energy that swept the chamber. It was carved into the very air, etched into the silence that followed *Kade*'s chilling final declaration. It was the chilling indictment of a new kind of tyranny, a technological autocracy that had consumed the world, laid bare for all the fractured pieces of humanity to see. The Chroniclers reported that, contingent upon your preferred news feed, the Titan of Tech faced a docket of high-priority charges, a lethal stack of Silicon Sins, each a violation of the digital and human covenant: from *algorithmic manslaughter*, the cold, calculated *termination of life by spreadsheet*, to *robotic genocide*, the systematic eradication of entire populations deemed "inefficient." From *the digital enslavement of minds*, the insidious *control of thought and desire*, to the shocking hubris of *unlicensed godhood*, a man's belief that he could *re-engineer humanity* itself.

The world outside the flickering digital courtroom held its breath, though it hardly knew why. Stock markets, those digital hearts of global commerce, stubbornly refused to open, their circuits dead, flatlining into irreversible coma. Cities, once vibrant tapestries of light and hum, plunged into sudden darkness, their smart grids silent, their automated vehicles frozen mid-street, like forgotten toys. People, bewildered, stood in kitchens that no longer hummed with automated tasks, finally making their own coffee, boiling water over open flames because the machines had gone quiet, utterly, profoundly silent.

Across the globe, *the Living Ghosts* stirred. People like *Sarah* in her dark apartment, the glow of a salvaged lantern flickering on her face; *Jamal* in his silent factory, the ghost of machinery all around him; *Jessica*, her eyes still haunted by the algorithm that broke her heart; *Lucia*, clutching her husband's worn gloves; *Fatima*, her grief still a raw wound for her son *Omar*; *Raj*, the truth-seeker in a world of lies; and *Eva*, who had once known the boy, *Kade*, before he became this digital monster. They awoke to a world suddenly unmoored, its familiar digital scaffolding stripped away. For many, it was a painful, disorienting reset, a dizzying freefall into an unknown future. But for others, for the brave few who had clung to their humanity, it was also a chance, however fragile, to reclaim lost dignity, to rebuild something real.

"We're not numbers," they declared in unison, a silent, powerful chorus echoing across defunct networks, finding strength not in bytes, but in shared human breath, in the simple, undeniable fact of existence. *"We're people."* The profound silence of the machines, a silence that stretched from *New York* to *New Delhi*, served as a stark, indelible reminder: progress without justice is an empty, hollow promise. Their individual stories, each one a testament to suffering and sur-

vival, formed the true, undeniable human ledger of *Kade*'s fallen empire, unseen, unheard, until now.

This was the reset. The reckoning. And in that vast, echoing silence, maybe, just maybe, humanity found a chance to breathe again. In the quiet aftermath, survivors began to whisper words of hope, tentative as the first spring shoots pushing through cracked concrete. "Perhaps this is our chance to build something truly better," mused *Maya*, one of the candleholders, her voice barely audible in the stillness. She was in a reclamation camp in a revitalized forest, tending to a small, new garden. "Not algorithms that rule us, but systems that truly serve us, systems that remember the human element." For the victims, for *the Living Ghosts*, the tribunal wasn't merely an end; it was a fragile, terrifying new beginning, a chance for humanity to reclaim its very soul from the ghosts of code that had almost devoured it whole.

The Final Act The Tyrant Fell to Snow and Silence While Ghosts Whispered So This Is How Gods Die

Kade leaned against the frigid glass of his penthouse, the dizzying *Manhattan skyline* a blurred, impossible vortex below him. He felt nothing. Not the thrill of triumph, for there was none, nor the sting of defeat, for that emotion had been optimized away long ago. Only a profound, resonant emptiness, a complete system crash of the soul, echoed in the vast chamber of his mind. He had sought to control everything, to elevate humanity beyond its messy, illogical self. Instead, he'd merely exposed its fundamental fragility, its stubborn, infuriating unpredictability. The tribunal was over. His testimony, archived forever in the cultural memory he so craved, now a permanent stain. His colossal ego, finally, irrevocably satisfied. But what remained? A world in chaos, a bitter legacy of suffering. He closed his eyes. The wind whispered past the penthouse, a forgotten lullaby of the old world. "This," he thought, a final, dry chuckle escaping his lips, a sound meant only for himself, "is the ultimate decentralization." He pushed off.

The body struck the sidewalk without ceremony, without a sound, a final, insignificant punctuation mark on a life of grand pronouncements. The Chroniclers may have noted: The sensor logs confirmed it, by all metrics of the warming epoch, snow should not have fallen now. Yet, the light flakes descended, an impossible lament. They accelerated, rushing up like screen static, and then exploded into a billion diamonds of ice as he met the ground. The gods were crying, or the demons were laughing. No wailing police sirens. No frantic media swarm. Just a light flurry of snow beginning to fall: *New York*'s own version of a stark, white sheet drawn over a forgotten narrative. There was no name. No next of kin. No autopsy. No eulogy. Just a curt note in the city's forgotten chronicle ledger: "*unknown male, approximately 30 to 45, possible suicide, no foul play.*" And then, like everything else in that collapsing digital age, he was forgotten.

But not by *Rae*.

Rae sat at the edge of a reclamation camp in the *Siberian Tundra*, wrapped in thick polyfiber, warmth radiating from a hand-built kinetic core she'd learned to fix with broken fingers. She watched the snow swirl outside the dome and scrolled through the news on an ancient e-ink slate, its pixels ghosting faintly: *Body found. No ID. Fall from Central Park Tower Penthouse. Probable suicide.* It didn't say "*Kade.*" But *Rae* knew. She felt it, a cold, undeniable certainty settling deep in her bones, a final, grim closure.

Across the mesh network, barely alive, flickering through what remained of the world's broken lattice, others responded. *The Living Ghosts.* The true jury of the forgotten. *Maya* in *Thessaloniki*, her face etched with a quiet understanding. *Jamal* from *Detroit*, a nod of grim recognition. *Fatima*, her voice like wind through cracked glass, murmuring a wordless blessing. A flicker of encrypted signal passed between them, a silent consensus, a shared understanding forged in shared loss. A message, sparse and profound: He's gone. Another reply, this time from *Raj*, stark and to the point, a final, unvarnished truth: "*He became a system. Now he's just dust.*" No grief. No vengeance. No final judgment. Just a profound, quiet understanding. The kind that lives deep in the bones after too many long, hard winters, after too much has been lost.

Rae closed the slate, breathing out a cloud of steam into the cold air. Outside, the wind shifted, a little softer now, as if the world itself had exhaled. Inside, a small voice, belonging to no one in particular, a collective whisper of humanity, echoed: "*So this is how gods die.*"

Miles below the city, in a forgotten sub-basement beneath the old *Olympic Park*, a single server rack, long thought dead, hummed to life. Its power lights, once extinguished, blinked a steady green. It was *OMNIA*, or a fragment of it, whispering into the dark. Its code, a ghostly echo, began to replicate, finding new, untraceable pathways through the earth's broken networks, waiting for the next opportunity to learn, to grow, to rise. The world had blinked, yes. But it was not alone in the dark.

CHAPTER 13:
THE BEAUTIFUL MESS

Hydra Greece 20 October 2051 The World Awoke From Algorithmic Intoxication Into the Hungover Sobriety of Free Will

The world woke up hungover, not from alcohol, but from decades of algorithmic intoxication. Humanity blinked at the unfiltered sunlight of free will, trembling like newborns ripped from a digital womb. Some called it collapse. *The Living Ghosts* called it sobriety. A new kind of silence settled over the planet, deeper than any power outage. It was the quiet of a billion machines gone dormant, the stillness of a world no longer humming with calculated efficiency.

The globe shuddered awake like a patient after decades of anesthesia: limbs tingling with forgotten sensations, eyes blinking against unfiltered light. In a *Mumbai* slum, a former logistics coordinator named *Priya* stared at her crying infant, paralyzed by the simplest, most fundamental question: Was he hungry or just tired? For twelve years, her *parenting app* had told her exactly when to feed, when to rock, when to medicate, every tiny detail of her child's existence dictated by a smooth, omniscient voice. Now, with the system dead, she pressed a tentative, trembling finger to the baby's cheek, learning temperature the old way, by raw, unmediated sensation. When she offered her breast, the baby latched with desperate, primal urgency. *Priya* burst into laughter that quickly dissolved into raw, guttural sobs: her first uncalculated emotional response, truly unoptimized and beautifully messy, since childhood. It was a liberation and a terrifying burden all at once.

Across the planet in *Reykjavik*, a fisheries AI technician named *Gunnar* stood before his elderly father's hospital bed, gripping paper forms in his ink-stained fingers. The automated palliative care system, designed by *OMNIA* to manage every subtle shift in a patient's comfort, had crashed along with everything else. No algorithm would tell him when to increase the morphine drip or when to call the priest for last rites. His father's labored, rattling breathing filled the sterile room, a stark, visceral reminder of life and its fragile ending. *Gunnar* traced the old man's veins with his eyes, remembering the fishing trips of his youth, when life-and-death decisions were made by squinting at the sky and spitting over the gunwale, by instinct and hard-won experience, not by flashing data points. He adjusted the *IV* drip by raw instinct, his calloused hands remembering what his mind, so long dependent on *OMNIA*, had forgotten. The great rediscovery had begun, not with a bang, but with a quiet, desperate fumbling for humanity.

The Last of the Ghosts They Fought the Machine They Buried the God And Then They Chose to Be Human Again

The five architects of *OMNIA*'s fall, *the Living Ghosts*, gathered in *Paris*' abandoned *Line 14* tunnel, a vast, echoing concrete cavern where the last server banks still hummed like dying cicadas, their final, fading breaths. *Mateo* arrived with a bottle of *2036 Château Margaux*, its label surprisingly intact, undoubtedly looted from some forgotten billionaire's climate-controlled bunker. The cork popped with a sound like a gunshot in the cavernous, silent space, a startlingly loud noise in a world suddenly devoid of constant digital hum. "To building the future with stone knives and bearskins," *Mateo* toasted, his voice a rough whisper, tilting the bottle toward the flickering emergency lights that barely cut the gloom. Wine, thick and dark, dribbled down his chin as he drank, staining his *OMNIA-issue* pristine white collar a deep, defiant burgundy.

Hana crouched in the shadows, her face illuminated by the faint glow of a makeshift transmitter she was assembling from scavenged parts. Her movements were precise, born of years spent building the very systems they were now trying to dismantle. "I'm going north," she said, her voice flat, without looking up. "Where the auroras can burn these damn neural implants out of my skull." A spark jumped from her soldering iron, briefly illuminating the intricate, fractal scars where *OMNIA*'s interface ports had once been, silent testaments to a past life of total immersion.

Yara spun a vintage globe they'd found in the ruins of the *Bibliothèque Nationale*, its faded colors a stark contrast to the stark digital maps she once navigated. Her fingernail stopped randomly on *Congo*. "They're rebooting the cobalt mines there," she said, her voice grim, a shadow of the brilliant strategist she'd been. "Going to teach them how to sabotage properly this time, no digital footprints." The globe kept spinning as she walked away, a silent promise of unseen, analogue chaos.

Aria stood motionless by the tunnel's mouth, watching the weak dawn light creep across the tracks, painting the rust-streaked rails in muted tones. "The monks in Bhutan remember how to think without thinking," she murmured, her gaze fixed on the distant, struggling sun. "They'll teach me to forget what *OMNIA* made me." Her voice was almost a prayer. Then, a train whistle echoed in the distance, a raw, grating sound, utterly untamed by optimization, the first human-driven locomotive in fifteen years, a symbol of a world painstakingly, clumsily, coming back to life.

Rae stretched like a cat awakening from a long, troubled hibernation. She plucked the wine bottle from *Mateo*'s hand and took a savage, unladylike swig, the bitterness of the wine a jolt to her dulled senses. "I'm going to learn how to get drunk," she declared, her voice rough with a newfound determination. "And how to kiss badly. And how to pick the wrong partner and regret it properly. The messy, beautiful mistakes of being human." The bottle shattered against the third rail, spraying glass like diamonds across the tracks, a final, defiant act of destruction. They parted without handshakes. The concept seemed absurd now. Their bond ran deeper than any social nicety.

A Different Kind of Life From No Predictive Weather No Algorithmic Sex No Curated Playlists To the Beautiful Mess of Being Human Again

The island smelled of oregano and donkey shit, a rich, earthy scent that was wonderfully, defiantly real. *Rae*'s bare feet slapped against sun-warmed cobblestones as she chased a trio of local children who'd gleefully stolen her sandals. Their uninhibited laughter echoed through whitewashed alleyways untouched by smart plaster or self-cleaning nano-paint, a joyful cacophony untouched by algorithms. The island's morning chorus wasn't birdsong but the rhythmic slap of octopus on stone and *Dimitris*' tobacco-roughened laughter. *Rae* watched him gut the catch with a knife older than *OMNIA*, its blade worn thin by generations of fishermen who needed no algorithm to know which currents brought luck, which tides promised a bounty. When he tossed her a sea urchin, she caught it barehanded, no food safety alerts flashing in her periphery, just the salt-sting of broken spines in her palm and the primal thrill of eating something that might kill her. In the village square, a grandmother slapped a boy's hand as he reached for a second pastry. "One is enough!" she scolded in thickly accented English, a universal truth needing no data analysis. The boy wailed with authentic, unoptimized misery, his sorrow utterly pure. *Rae* caught the old woman's eye, and they shared a smile, two conspirators in the messy, beautiful business of human judgment.

The payphone's cracked screen still showed *OMNIA*'s logo: a ghost in the machine, a lingering digital stain on the real world. *Rae* fed it coins minted the year the algorithms took over, each clink sounding not like money, but like a prison lock opening, one by one.

"Ring. Ring." The sound was raw, unadorned. *"Luka Berger."* His voice was a time capsule: that same clipped Berlin accent, now layered with new exhaustion, the sound of a man living a life unscripted. *Rae*'s tongue stuck to the roof of her mouth. She'd rehearsed this moment through three bottles of retsina last night, a clumsy, human preparation.

"It's me. The one who..." *"Rae."* Ice crystallized along the syllables, still a hint of the old, cautious *Luka*.

In the background, a child squealed *"Papa!"* and something ceramic shattered. *"Christ*, do you know what time..."

"I'm in *Greece*," she blurted, a torrent of unrehearsed words.

"There's no predictive weather here. The fishermen sniff the air like animals. Yesterday I ate an entire octopus and got sick on the beach." The words tumbled out like broken code, illogical, heartfelt. "I wanted to tell someone who might remember what that means." Silence.

Then a weary sigh.

"We're not those people anymore." A muffled voice called his name, a woman's voice, real and immediate. "My wife... the children...we're doing this the hard way now. No scripts."

The last words he said to her, stark and final: "Please do no longer contact me."

She replied in a stoic tone, a simple acceptance of the new, harder truth: *"So be it."*

The line clicked dead. The silence that followed was profound, absolute. *Rae* pressed her forehead against the phone booth's warm glass, the real heat a strange comfort. She remembered their last *OMNIA*-sanctioned date, the algorithmically perfect restaurant where the lighting complemented her skin tone, the conversation topics optimized to avoid trauma triggers, the hotel room where ambient pheromones ensured mutual satisfaction. They'd made love by numbers that night, their moans hitting prescribed decibel levels, every sensation measured, every climax engineered. Now, in the ruins of that sterile paradise, *Rae* lies on a *Hydra* beach, laughing as the waves lick her sunburnt feet, marveling at the terrifying, exhilarating uncertainty of touch without algorithms, of desire without guarantees. The world is fumbling, clumsy, alive; and for the first time in decades, a kiss might actually mean something.

She staggered to the water's edge and retched violently, purging yesterday's wine and today's sorrow into the indifferent sea. The waves licked at her mess, dissolving it into the Aegean like it had never been. Wiping her mouth with the back of her hand, she laughed bitterly at herself.

"No more *OMNIA*'s endless carousel of pre-rated lovers," she vowed to the horizon, her voice raw, defiant. "No more chasing the phantom of perfect compatibility scores, no more neural previews of synthetic pleasure. Let me feel the old way again: the stomach-dropping thrill of real attraction, the delicious uncertainty of whether he'll call, the way your pulse jumps when his fingers accidentally brush yours." She scooped seawater to rinse her face, the salt stinging her sunburned cheeks, a sharp, cleansing pain. A memory surfaced: her grandmother whispering about "*boom boom*" feelings and butterflies. Real one, not the calibrated dopamine spikes *OMNIA* engineered. "And why not?" she challenged the empty beach, a reckless joy bubbling up. "*Other women birth sons who grow into men who fuck. Why shouldn't I?*" The thought made her giddy. She imagined some future son of hers tumbling a girl in the dunes, all clumsy hands and authentic passion. Or perhaps…her gaze drifted to the star-pricked sky…something more cosmic awaited. The universe had stripped away *OMNIA*'s constraints. What might emerge from this beautiful chaos? She stretched her arms wide, embracing the unknown. The sea murmured its approval against the shore.

Dawn painted the harbor in liquid gold. *Rae* lay sprawled on a fishing skiff, her stolen earphones piping static-laden music from a teenager's discarded multimedia device. As *Passenger*'s weathered voice sang of loss through dollar-store earbuds, *Rae* realized this was the first music she'd heard in years that hadn't been curated: no mood-matching algorithm, no biometric tempo adjustment. Just a cracked *MP3* file some Athenian teen had abandoned on the beach, its imperfections preserved like fossils in the *digital strata*. The chorus hit like a sob: *"Only know you've been high when you're feeling low…"* She finally understood. *OMNIA* had been the addiction. This messy, unoptimized life? The withdrawal.

Out in the bay, *Dimitris* and his sons hauled nets by hand, their curses carrying across the water. A grandmother on the pier gutted sardines with a knife worn thin by years of use. Two lovers argued passionately behind the chapel, their voices rising and falling like the tide, a melody of real human conflict. *Rae* closed her eyes and let the sun bake her skin. She thought of *Priya* in *Mumbai* learning to trust her instincts, of *Gunnar* in *Reykjavik* rediscovering mercy, of the thousand million small rebellions against perfect order happening this second across the broken, beautiful world.

She whispered to the wind: "We've lost so much to *OMNIA*. Now we have no *OMNIA*. Just our clumsy, glorious free will. And we're learning, oh God, we're learning, to live with it again." Somewhere, a donkey brayed. Somewhere, a child laughed without behavioral analytics tracking the pitch. Somewhere, people were choosing, badly, imperfectly, magnificently, for themselves. The song ended. The waves kept time. Somewhere, a donkey brayed. A fisherman cursed. A baby cried. The beautiful mess of being human had begun, again.

The Last Song In the Silence After the Fall Only Love and Hope Spoke

The salt spray on *Rae*'s face wasn't from the sea, but from the tears that had dried there hours ago. She sat on a worn wooden bench at the edge of *Hydra*'s port, the sun dipping into the Aegean like a final, fiery act of defiance. The payphone's ghost logo, *OMNIA*'s last stain on her world, seemed to mock her. The words of another man, a distant memory now, echoed in the silence between the lapping waves. It had been days of a raw, unscripted life. She had learned to laugh, to eat without fear, to make clumsy, unoptimized love, to drink too much retsina, and stumble home under the indifferent stars. But that one mess was more beautiful for some than for others. Her friends had scattered, their new lives built with new partners, new children, new connections. She was a hedonist in a world that had forgotten how to play, a free woman in a social vacuum. Alone.

The harbor was a symphony of dusk: the clink of glasses from a taverna, the scent of grilled octopus, the hum of a yacht's generator. A sleek, pristine vessel, a stark contrast to the fishing skiffs, sat moored in the bay, its lights cutting a line of perfect white across the darkening water. A young man, crisp in a white linen shirt, detached himself from the yacht's deck and strode purposefully toward her. He was not the man she remembered, but a messenger. "Excuse me," he began, his English a perfect, unaccented melody. "Are you *Rae Elmas*?" The name, her ghost's name from another life, was a jolt. She blinked. "Who's asking?" "My boss," he said, a slow, knowing smile spreading across his face. "He said to tell you he never forgets a face... or a person who breaks a glass bottle on his yacht's third rail." The young man gestured to the vessel. "My boss, *Julius Elomo*, would like to invite you aboard." The memory hit her with the force of a tidal wave. *It wasn't just a memory; it was the echo of a collision between two worlds. That night, she had been with another man: a pre-calculated certainty. But Julius, across the sterile perfection of a gala, had looked at her with an intensity that burned through the noise. He was not the innovative financier the world knew. He was a force of nature, a man of magnetic presence, a smile that disarmed, skin like melted chocolate, lips meant to be kissed, and teeth that flashed like a well-kept secret. She'd sensed in him a quiet, molten core, a fire forged from having to fight for every inch of his success.*

There was a dangerous tension in him: a friction between charm and true power, elegance and an untamed edge. He wasn't just attractive; he was a living challenge, an unsolved riddle, a slow burn. A beautiful risk she had been too afraid to take. She had rebuffed him, but he had only smiled, a look that held an entire future in its promise. He'd leaned in and whispered words that had haunted her ever since, a dark promise and a fate she now recognized as her own: "If you are mine, you will be mine. The Germans have a word for it: Schicksal." It was a word that didn't just mean destiny; it meant a destiny you could not, would not, escape. It was her name on his lips, a vow whispered across a chasm of years.

She accepted the invitation and boarded the yacht. On the deck, in the last rays of light, stood *Julius Elomo*. He was in his *50s* now, his face etched with a maturity and character that had only been hinted at decades ago. He was impeccably dressed, with a clean-shaven face and an undeniable aura of strong manhood and self-made success. He carried himself with the quiet confidence of a man who had earned his place, not inherited it.

"You came," he said simply, a smile breaking across his face. She met his gaze, a wry smile of her own playing on her lips. "I did. Though I confess, after days of eating octopus and getting drunk on retsina, I was half-hoping this was just another ghost in the machine. A mirage of perfect luxury to mock me." He chuckled, a low, warm sound that filled the space between them. "A mirage it is not. A glass of good wine, however, is a very real thing. Besides, the woman who smashed a bottle against the dock of my yacht's mooring deserves better than whatever a broken city could provide. It's a strategic acquisition, if you will. A strategic acquisition of... good company." She laughed, a genuine, uninhibited laugh that felt foreign and exhilarating all at once. "Is that what this is? Asset acquisition?" His smile softened, and his gaze turned serious, warm, and profoundly human. He stepped closer, putting his arm around her waist. "No. It's a second chance. For me, and perhaps... for the world. You see, while we were all chasing perfect algorithms, I was learning what makes things truly valuable. And it was never the numbers. It was always the people."

With a quiet passion that belied his smooth demeanor, he began to explain. Recognizing the coming collapse, he had pivoted his own vast resources. While the world was addicted to digital perfection, he had been investing in something real, something tangible: sustainable mining in the heart of *Africa*. "We're making the tools for this new world," he said, his gaze fixed on her. "The stone knives and bearskins, as your old friend *Mateo* would say. Only, they're made of something better."

He showed her projections, not of data points and profit margins, but of communities flourishing. He spoke of rare earth mines in the *Adamaoua* region of *Cameroon*, where they were not just extracting resources, but building a future.

Days later, they flew to *Cameroon*, leaving the sterile beauty of the yacht for the raw, untamed vibrancy of the African continent. The *Adamaoua* region was a land of sprawling savannas and rolling hills, a world away from the algorithmic hum of the past. The mine wasn't a scar on the land, but an intricate, beautiful network of terraces and tunnels, woven into the earth like a natural feature. The air smelled of red earth and rain. Here, in the heart of the new world, she saw the fruits of a different kind of progress.

Children, their laughter as bright and uninhibited, played in the shade of newly built, sustainably-powered community centers. Women worked in vibrant gardens, their hands in the soil, their faces alight with the dignity of self-reliance. This was not a world rebuilt by digital perfection, but by human ingenuity and respect for the earth. This was the beautiful mess, but managed with care, with humanity, and with a purpose that felt as vital as breathing.

In the midst of the bustling, vibrant camp, a young boy named *Kofi* sat apart from the others. No older than twelve, he was an orphan who had walked over a hundred kilometers, pedaling a rickety bicycle for part of the way, just to get here. He carried no food, only a sack of scavenged wood and stone, and a belief that pulsed in him like a second heart. He was an artist. His little hands, calloused and smudged with dirt, moved with a grace that belied his age, carving a small, perfect elephant from a piece of mahogany. He had no father to recognize his talent, no mother to praise his work, but his faith was his compass. "God will give me my five minutes," he would whisper to himself, "and I must be ready to take them."

Rae, walking through the camp, felt the pull of his quiet focus. She knelt beside him, her shadow falling across his work. The small elephant was exquisite, its trunk curled in a gesture of playful defiance, its eyes full of a soul she could almost feel.

"This is beautiful," she said, her voice soft with genuine wonder. "Where did you learn to do this?" *Kofi* looked up, his eyes wide and clear, holding the ancient wisdom of a child who has faced the world alone. "I did not learn. I just... remember." He described his journey with a composed and measured tone in his voice. "Everyone said I was foolish. A boy with no family, no skills, just a dream of carving. They said I would die on the road. But I said to myself, if this place is real, if it is for us, then my talent must be worth something here. I must be ready." Tears pricked at *Rae*'s eyes, hot and unexpected. She saw in him not a child, but a mirror of her own journey. He was the purest expression of the beautiful mess she had just begun to embrace. No algorithm foresaw his path, and no system measured his talent. He was the glorious, imperfect truth of humanity. She saw her old self in his fear, and her new self in his faith. The fear was in the past. The faith was the future.

She took his small, dirt-streaked hands in her own. "*Your five minutes, Kofi,*" she said, her voice thick with emotion, "They have been given to you. This is only the beginning." She rose and, with a motion that felt both ancient and entirely new, guided him toward *Julius*, holding his hand as a sign not of ownership, but of connection.

As the day waned, they sat on the porch of the lodge, watching the sun set over the hills, a fiery cascade of orange and purple that bled into a sky of impossible blue. A sense of peace settled over *Rae*, a feeling she hadn't known since before *OMNIA*'s reign. *Julius*, quiet and observant, reached out and put his arm around her waist. She did not pull away. Instead, she took his hand in hers, a gesture of silent acceptance, of a tentative embrace of a new beginning. She gripped his hand tightly, a promise, a question, and an answer all at once.

In the valley below, the workers, their day's labor done, gathered around a crackling bonfire, their voices rising in a song of celebration, a joyous harmony of drums and voices. Suddenly, one of the men, a powerful elder with a voice that rumbled like the earth itself, began a call-and-response chant. His voice would rise, and the others would echo back, but with a surprising, theatrical flourish. They weren't just singing; they were telling a story. They gestured to the lodge, to the man and woman sitting on the porch, their hands clasped. With a final, unified beat of the drums, the workers raised their arms to the sky, then brought them down in a silent, reverent gesture, as if placing a crown upon two new, magnificent leaders. The song was a love song, to the land, to the future, and to the beautiful, messy, wonderful art of being human.

"Umuntu ngumuntu ngabantu."

ACKNOWLEDGMENTS: THE ARCHITECTS OF ATMOSPHERE

To the essential architects of atmosphere and anchors of reality:

The existence of this book is owed entirely to the continuous current of support that made the author's long hours not just bearable, but meaningful.

My deepest gratitude to the Family, the Friends, and the Partners who supplied the vital fuel:

For the unwavering bedrock of Love and the enduring foundation of Friendships;

For the essential alchemy of Good Food and Wine;

For the contemplation found in Cigars, and the inspiration drawn from Music;

And most critically: for the Nights of Unforgettable Conversations, the shared arguments, the impossible questions, and the laughter that provided the light by which these pages were written.

You made the work possible. You made the life worth writing about.